Samuel French Acting Edition

Sandy Toes
& Salty Kisses

by Michael Parker &
Susan Parker

SAMUELFRENCH.COM   SAMUELFRENCH.CO.UK

FOR PRODUCTION ENQUIRIES

UNITED STATES AND CANADA
Info@SamuelFrench.com
1-866-598-8449

UNITED KINGDOM AND EUROPE
Plays@SamuelFrench.co.uk
020-7255-4302

Each title is subject to availability from Samuel French, depending upon country of performance. Please be aware that *SANDY TOES & SALTY KISSES* may not be licensed by Samuel French in your territory. Professional and amateur producers should contact the nearest Samuel French office or licensing partner to verify availability.

MUSIC USE NOTE

Licensees are solely responsible for obtaining formal written permission from copyright owners to use copyrighted music in the performance of this play and are strongly cautioned to do so. If no such permission is obtained by the licensee, then the licensee must use only original music that the licensee owns and controls. Licensees are solely responsible and liable for all music clearances and shall indemnify the copyright owners of the play(s) and their licensing agent, Samuel French, against any costs, expenses, losses and liabilities arising from the use of music by licensees. Please contact the appropriate music licensing authority in your territory for the rights to any incidental music.

IMPORTANT BILLING AND CREDIT REQUIREMENTS

If you have obtained performance rights to this title, please refer to your licensing agreement for important billing and credit requirements.

SANDY TOES & SALTY KISSES was first produced in the United States by The Ritz Company Players at The Waterfront at Silver Birches, Hawley, Pennsylvania on February 9, 2018. The director was Sandy Gabrielson and the designer was Sarah Clauss. The cast was as follows:

CANDY . . . . Sarah Lehman

WILBERFORCE "BUBBA" BROWN . . . . Pete Pettinato

AUDRINA BROWN . . . . Caroline Lehman

BEATRICE RUTHERFORD-SMYTHE . . . . .Molly Rodgers

TRACI RUTHERFORD-SMYTHE . . . . Chiara Marone

DOUGLAS DUPONT . . . . Mark Zimmer

PETER MUDD . . . . Richard Nadolski

CHARACTERS

CANDY – (Age 25+) A local gal, who is working so she can put herself through college. She is vivacious, and personable, all of which make her eminently suitable for her job as the hotel receptionist. She enjoys her job, and although she appears to be a bit of a "flake," her innocent, good-natured and quirky personality always shines through to cover her inadequacies. Candy's innate, innocent ability to make a mess of things causes many comedic visual sequences, which involve her, and therefore she needs to be reasonably agile and athletic.

WILLBERFORCE "BUBBA" BROWN – (Age 50+) Bubba is the younger brother of Archibald Brown, the former "recently deceased" owner of the hotel. He is rough around the edges, ingenious, and has a heart of gold. He has been the maintenance and operations manager of the hotel for many years. We learn, as the play progresses that most of these operations are unconnected with the daily running of the hotel, and are highly illegal. Bubba, however, seems to have found a way around the illegalities (*at least in his own mind*). When Madame Coco, the wedding planner suddenly elopes, he is coerced by his niece into playing her role. A series of quick changes have the Rutherford-Smythe's believing that there really is a very "eccentric" Madame Coco.

AUDRINA BROWN – (Age 30+) The late Archibald's daughter and Bubba's niece, grew up in the hotel, but has not been there very much since graduating high school. She inherited the property a few weeks ago and has very recently taken over the business end of running the hotel. She is efficient, resourceful, smart and practical. She quickly learns that this hotel does not run like any other businesses with which she has been involved. As a loving and doting niece, she is faced with the problem of Uncle Bubba. Is he a "Good ol' Southern boy," or a crafty criminal?

BEATRICE RUTHERFORD-SMYTHE – (Age 50+) She belongs to what the authors call "The American Aristocracy," the so-called blue bloods of New England. She is more concerned with her perspective son-in-law's family history and background than anything else about him. She has a superior attitude, which tends to annoy people with whom she comes into contact. She is very used to dominating those around her and likes things done her way. As the play progresses she adapts to the casual lifestyle of Lovers' Landing and ironically finds herself attracted to Bubba, a man who is the total antithesis of everything in her life.

TRACI RUTHERFORD-SMYTHE – (Age 25+) Beatrice's daughter has selected the Lovers' Landing Beach Hotel for her destination wedding, probably to avoid the socialite trappings upon which her mother would otherwise insist. She is marrying Peter, whom she has known for only a short time, despite the fact that her mother considers him totally unsuitable. At first we see her as a self-centered, pampered, rich girl. But, as she discovers what she thinks is her fiancé's apparent infidelity, she becomes a strong-minded woman, determined to discover the truth.

DOUGLAS DUPONT – (Age 30+) Checks into the hotel and arouses Bubba's suspicions when he is found taking detailed photographs of the hotel and asking questions of the locals in town. Bubba believes him to be a government agent from the Bureau of Alcohol Tobacco, Firearms and Explosives. Audrina, agrees to help her Uncle discover who he is, but in doing so, begins to fall for Douglas. Candy innocently mistakes him for Peter Mudd causing Douglas a great deal of trouble. While investigating the hotel, he becomes convinced that there is some truth to the mystique of Lovers' Landing, the home of sandy toes and salty kisses, especially after Candy, Traci, Audrina, Beatrice, and yes even Madame Coco "come on to him." It isn't till the end of the play that it is revealed he is a writer for a destination wedding magazine. *(This role can be doubled with the actor also playing Peter Mudd.) [SEE AUTHORS' NOTES.]*

PETER MUDD – (Age 30+) Traci's fiancé arrives at Lovers' Landing, and despite his rocky relationship with his future mother-in-law, the dragon lady, he is looking forward to spending time with his lovely bride to be. Alas, poor Peter never gets that chance. One event after another, created accidentally by Candy, leaves Peter in compromising positions. Beatrice and Traci, believing he has "strayed," purposely render him unconscious. Despite the on again-off again wedding, Peter continues to try to convince Traci of his love.

SETTING

The Lovers' Landing Beach Hotel
Southern USA, on the Gulf of Mexico

ACT I   A Friday morning in summer
ACT II   Later the same day

The reception area of Lovers' Landing Beach Hotel located on a barrier
island on the Gulf of Mexico in the Southern USA

ACT I   Mid-morning
ACT II   Later the same day

TIME

The Present

ACT I

(The curtain rises on an empty set. It is the reception area of Lovers' Landing Beach Hotel. Situated immediately back of the beach the hotel, while clearly quite old, has a rustic charm and warmth which attracts locals and tourists alike. Over the years it has become ever more popular as a wedding destination, and the owners have added a wedding chapel, tiki hut style, right on the beach itself. The furniture is tropical, ideally white wicker or rattan with colorful cushions. The décor is "beachy" and / or nautical. Down right by the entrance is a self-standing sign, made out of or made to look like drift wood. [SEE AUTHORS' DRAWING.] Below it is a shoe tray with miscellaneous flip flops. The open entrance down right leads to the hotel entrance and the parking lot. Above it, on the right wall is a novelty bar or drinks trolley. On it is an ice bucket, several small sample glasses and a pitcher of "barracudas," the signature rum punch drink of the hotel. Up right is a reception counter with a call bell and both a cell phone and a land line on a cradle on it. Behind the counter, to the right is an open archway to the office. On the upstage wall is a double hinged, spring loaded door to the kitchen, with an "employees only" sign on it. To the left of the kitchen door on the wall are two decorative oars. On the left is a couch, a low backed easy chair, and a coffee table with a couple of magazines. On the left

wall above the furniture is the door to room 7. Above room 7 is a hallway leading to the other hotel rooms. Below the furniture of the left wall is the frame work of sliding glass doors to the beach, which are always open.)

*(The phone is ringing as **CANDY** enters from the office. She is cheerful and personable. She is dressed casually wearing a wrap around skirt, a "V" neck blouse, a slip or lacy undergarments, flip flops, and simple jewelry.)*

CANDY. *(Picks up the cell phone.)* Hello, *(The phone continues to ring.)* Hello. *(The phone continues to ring. She holds the phone away and looks at it. The phone continues to ring. She rolls her eyes as if to say "silly me" then places the phone to her other ear.)* Hello. *(The phone continues to ring. Finally she has it figured out. She abandons the cell phone and picks up the land line.)* Hello, Lovers' Landing Beach Hotel, the home of sandy toes and salty kisses. This is Candy, how can I help you? *(Pauses.)* Yes, of course, we are known for our destination weddings. We even have a little wedding chapel right on the beach. Well, actually it looks like a tiki hut, and I suppose it really is a tiki hut, but it's adorable as a wedding chapel. *(Pauses.)* Oh, I'm afraid you're going to have to discuss dates and availability with our wedding planner, Madame Coco. We often get booked months in advance. Let me get your name and number, *(Grabs a piece of paper and a pen and starts to write.)* Oh, oh, oh, just a minute, I can't get the pen to work. *(She holds up the pen and shakes it then realizes she didn't take the cap off. She takes off the cap.)* Okay, go ahead Ms. Block, *(Pauses.)* What? Could you please spell that for me. *(She begins to write.)* B-L-A-C-K, Oh, Ms. Black, that's funny because the hotel owner's name is Brown, and Madame Coco's is Coco. I don't have a color for my last name. *(Pauses.)* Sorry, right, I've got your number. I will make sure that Madame Coco returns your call. *(Pauses.)* Well, she's rather busy this weekend, so it may be Monday before she gets back to you. *(Pauses.)* Thank you and have a great day. *(Hangs up.)*

> *(Enter* **BUBBA** *from up left. He is wearing swim trunks, t-shirt and full scuba diving gear. He has swim fins on his feet (the longer, the better), an air tank on his back, his mask is perched on top of his head and he holds the regulator mouthpiece in one hand. He takes a few very awkward steps right then stops.)*

Mr. Brown is that you?

BUBBA. No, it's a Portuguese sumo wrestler.

CANDY. *(Moving out from behind the counter.)* Why are you dressed... *(She stops suddenly and then holds her nose.)* Whoa, whoa, back off. What is that horrible smell? *(Begins to back away.)*

BUBBA. The septic tank got clogged up again and I had to fix it.

CANDY. You went scuba diving in the septic tank?

BUBBA. Yeah, well the valve to the drain field got stuck. *(He takes a step towards her.)*

CANDY. Ugh, that's gross. *(She takes one step back, reaches under the counter to grab a spray can of air freshener. Holding it at arm's length, she sprays* **BUBBA**, *who backs away.)* Does this happen often?

BUBBA. It's not that bad, I've already hosed myself off, and anyway, it's all over now.

CANDY. It's all over everywhere! *(She continues to spray the air as* **BUBBA** *backs away left.)*

BUBBA. Oh come on, a bit of muck won't hurt you. Now, can you help me get these fins off?

CANDY. You want me to touch those fins? Just a minute. *(She puts the air freshener on the counter and rushes into the kitchen.)*

BUBBA. Now where are you going? I swear that girl moves faster than a chicken on a June bug.

CANDY. *(Reappears immediately putting on a pair of big yellow rubber gloves. She approaches* **BUBBA** *tentatively, her arms outstretched and her head turned away. She stops and straightens up.)* I want a pay raise.

BUBBA. Girl, you're nuttier than a fruitcake. Never mind, I'll get it off myself. *(Starts to move right towards the office, but stops before entering.)* Oh, I almost forgot why I came in here. Could you please tell Audrina I haven't forgotten our meeting this morning and I'll get with her just as soon as I've cleaned up. *(Exits to office.)*

CANDY. *(She takes off the yellow gloves and sets them on the counter.)* I'm nuttier than a fruitcake? Who went swimming in the septic tank? *(She gives another spray as the phone rings. She reaches for the cell phone, catches herself, smiles and picks up the other one.)* Hello, Lovers' Landing Beach Hotel, home of sandy toes and salty kisses, *(Holds the phone away from her.)* and screwball scuba divers. *(Listens into the phone again.)* How can I help you? *(Pauses.)* Oh, I'm so sorry to have to tell you, but Mr. Archibald Brown, the owner of the hotel passed away a couple of weeks ago. His daughter Audrina is the new owner. *(Pauses.)* Is who still here? There's no one here by – oh, you must mean Bubba, oh yes, he's still here. *(Pauses.)* Okay, I'll have him call you. *(Hangs up.)*

AUDRINA. *(Enters from down right. She is wearing a casual dress or skirt and blouse, with sandals, simple jewelry. She moves up to the left side of the reception counter.)* Good morning Candy, it's a beautiful day isn't it.

CANDY. Yes Miss Brown, it certainly is.

AUDRINA. Candy, you've been calling me that since I arrived three days ago.

CANDY. I know, it's your name.

AUDRINA. I realize I'm your boss, but I'd really feel more comfortable if you'd call me Audrina.

CANDY. Yes Miss Brow..., I mean Audrina.

AUDRINA. So, what's on the schedule for today?

CANDY. *(Checks the computer.)* It looks like it's going to be a busy day. A Mrs. Beatrice Rutherford-Smythe and her daughter Traci, will be arriving any minute. They're here to check out the hotel for her daughter's wedding. They have a meeting scheduled with Madame Coco later this morning. The fiancé, Peter Mudd, is arriving too, but he didn't give a specific time. Oh, and a Mr. DuPont is checking in today as well. Is there anything special you need me to do to get ready for them?

AUDRINA. It looks like you have the rum punch barracuda drinks ready for our guests so I think we're all set. *(Pauses.)* Have you ever tried the barracudas here?

CANDY. No Ma'am, I don't go near that stuff.

AUDRINA. Why not?

CANDY. I know what's in them.

AUDRINA. *(Laughs.)* If Uncle Bubba makes them they can be deadly. By the way, have you seen him this morning?

CANDY. I almost forgot... *(She grabs the yellow gloves and quickly exits to the kitchen.)*

AUDRINA. Where are you going? If I didn't know better I'd swear that girl was a butterfly in another life.

CANDY. *(Re-enters with a bucket and mop and starts to wipe the floor where **BUBBA** was walking.)* I really don't know why he had to walk through here with his wet, stinky fins after diving into the septic tank. It's not like I don't have enough to do today, with guests checking in and...

AUDRINA. Candy, *(Not heard by **CANDY** who keeps mopping.)* Candy *(She walks over and taps **CANDY** on the shoulder. She immediately swings the mop around nearly hitting **AUDRINA** who has to duck.)* Ohh!

CANDY. *(Swinging the mop back around again, causing **AUDRINA** to have to duck.)* I'm so sorry, are you alright?

AUDRINA. Candy, I'll feel much safer if you would please put the mop down. *(**CANDY** places it in the bucket.)* Are you telling me that Uncle Bubba was swimming in the septic tank. Why?

CANDY. It needed fixing.

AUDRINA. *(Laughing.)* That sounds like something Uncle Bubba would do. He's been the maintenance man for this hotel ever since I was a little girl. Do you know where he is now? I was supposed to meet him for our daily briefing.

CANDY. That's right, I almost forgot, he told me to tell you he hasn't forgotten and will meet you as soon as he gets cleaned up.

AUDRINA. Okay. If you need me, I'll be in the kitchen. Here I'll take that. *(Picks up the mop and bucket and exits to kitchen.)*

> *(**CANDY** sniffs the air then picks up the air freshener, gives it a spray then exits to the office. Enter **BEATRICE** and **TRACI** from down right.)*

> *(**BEATRICE**, in manner, bearing, attitude and appearance is clearly a member of New England's social elite. Everything about her creates the impression of arrogance and superiority. She is wearing a sleeveless blouse with a blazer, dress pants or skirt, dress pumps or heels, a pearl necklace and earrings, and a watch. Her hair should be up in a French roll. Her outfit and appearance should state, "I'm an aristocrat and have money." She is carrying a purse. She is followed by her daughter **TRACI** who is the product of her mother's world, and while she does not subscribe to the snobbishness of that world, she nevertheless appears to be self-centered, shallow and pampered. She knows how to manipulate her mother to get her own way. She has selected The Lovers' Landing Beach Hotel for her destination*

> *wedding despite her mother's objections. She is wearing a sleeveless dress with a long scarf around her neck, heeled sandals with a purse. She should have a reasonably sized diamond on her hand, but not too large. Jewelry should look expensive, but elegant.)*

BEATRICE. *(Looking around as she moves up stage.)* Traci, I really can't understand why you want to have your wedding in this God forsaken shambles of a hotel. There isn't even a door man.

TRACI. *(Following her up stage.)* Mom, we've been all through this. I've told you that Peter's family would feel out of place at your country club, besides this place has a lot of charm.

BEATRICE. If shabby is your idea of charm, it certainly has an abundance of it.

TRACI. Mother, you always said I could have my wedding anywhere I wanted, and this is where I decided to have it, and anyway, Peter likes this place.

BEATRICE. Well he would, wouldn't he.

TRACI. And what's that suppose to mean?

BEATRICE. You know exactly what I mean. Now, let's check in. *(She steps towards the counter and taps the bell lightly. No one appears so she rings it again. No one appears.)* Traci, they don't even have anyone working the front desk. *(She starts to bang the bell loudly, and nonstop.)*

CANDY. *(Enters from the office and grabs the bell off the counter.)* Good morning, welcome to Lovers' Landing Beach Hotel. You must be the Smythes.

BEATRICE. *(Rolls her eyes.)* Absolutely not. I am Beatrice Rutherford-Smythe, *(Emphasis on Rutherford.)* and this is my daughter Traci.

CANDY. *(Puts the bell back on the counter.)* Gee, I've never met anyone who had two last names before.

BEATRICE. No, I don't suppose in a place like this you would. We wish to check in and I would like to know which room I'm in.

CANDY. You're in the reception room.

BEATRICE. *(Rolls her eyes.)* I meant which rooms will we be staying in?

CANDY. Well, we've set aside rooms seven, eight and nine. They're right on the beach.

BEATRICE. Adjacent?

CANDY. I don't know about that, but they are right next to each other.

BEATRICE. In that case, I will take room eight, Traci you can have room nine, and Peter can stay in room seven.

TRACI. *(Rolls her eyes, stomps her foot and whines.)* Mother, I don't know why I can't have the room next to Peter. It's not like I'm ten years old anymore.

BEATRICE. No, you're not, so I suggest you stop acting like it. This time you're not going to get your way. *(To* **CANDY.***)* Now that we have that settled, could you please have your bellman bring in our luggage.

CANDY. *(Handing* **BEATRICE** *the room key.)* Bellman?

BEATRICE. The person who brings our bags in from the car?

CANDY. Ohhh... That's usually Mr. Brown, he's our operations manager, but he's not available right now.

> *(***BEATRICE*** *looks at* **TRACI** *as if to say, "I told you so.")*

TRACI. Don't look at me, I'm not going to bring them in, it's way too hot out there.

BEATRICE. Of course you're not. *(Takes the keys out of her purse and hands them to* **CANDY.***)* You'll find the Mercedes in the parking lot.

CANDY. Oh, right. Please, help yourself to a complimentary sample of our speciality rum punch, the barracuda. I'll be right back. *(Exits down right.)*

BEATRICE. *(Now at the drinks table pouring two rum punches.)* You know this really is quite extraordinary.

I don't believe I've ever stayed anywhere where they served free alcohol at all times of the day. *(She hands* **TRACI** *a rum punch, crosses left and sits on the couch left side.)* Maybe they think it will make this place look better. Now Traci, come and sit down, I want to talk to you.

TRACI. I wonder why they call it a barracuda? *(Follows left and sits in the chair and takes a sip.)* Oh, *(Coughs.)* I think I know.

BEATRICE. *(Takes a sip and is about to set her glass down on the coffee table, but before she does she swipes her finger across the top as if checking for dust, then sets her glass down.)* Well at least the place is clean. *(Sniffs the air.)* Even if it does smell a bit like air freshener.

TRACI. Mother, I don't have all day, what is it you want to talk about?

BEATRICE. Well, before we meet with Madame Coco, is there any way that I can persuade you to call this wedding off?

TRACI. Mother, don't start that again.

BEATRICE. But Traci darling, I don't believe he's good enough for you.

TRACI. What's wrong with him?

BEATRICE. Well for a start his name.

TRACI. *(Rolls her eyes.)* Here we go again.

BEATRICE. You do realize that Traci Rutherford-Smythe is about to become Mrs. M-u-u-d-d. *(She says Mudd in a drawn out disdainful way and repeats it exactly that way every time she says it in the play.)*

CANDY. *(Appears down right.)* Excuse me, but what does a Mercedes look like?

BEATRICE. It's large, expensive, white, with personalized license plates, B-E-A rich.

CANDY. When I get out of college, I'm going to get me one of those. Excuse me. *(Exits down right.)*

TRACI. Mother, Peter is a very nice young man, and he treats me like a princess. I really don't think it matters what his name is.

BEATRICE. It's not just his name, what about his background, his lineage? Where in heaven's name did the Mudds come from? What's his ancestry?

TRACI. You make him sound like a puppy dog with a pedigree.

BEATRICE. There's a lot to be said for family background. It indicates a standard of integrity and upbringing. Both the Rutherfords and the Smythes have been outstanding citizens for nearly two hundred years. We are respected, we are trusted, we are pillars of society. Who is Peter Mudd?

TRACI. Mother, he's a lawyer.

BEATRICE. You make my point for me.

TRACI. Very funny. Mom, have I ever told you...

BEATRICE. No, and don't start now.

CANDY. *(Appears down right with the key in her hand and moves towards the chair.)* I'm sorry to interrupt, but I can't seem to find the keyhole to open the trunk.

BEATRICE. There is no keyhole. Traci, show her which button it is. *(**TRACI** stands and shows **CANDY** the button to push and moves back to her chair.)* Now young lady, do you suppose you can possibly manage to bring in our bags?

CANDY. I'll have them here in a jiffy. *(Exits down right.)*

BEATRICE. You know dear, there is still time to cancel this wedding, or at least postpone it. You've only known him for such a short time. You can't possibly know much about him. How can you be sure he's your Prince Charming? If your father was alive, he would have insisted on all sorts of background checks. He could be a serial killer for all you know.

TRACI. Mother, I've heard quite enough...

CANDY. *(Suddenly there is the continuous beeping of a horn alarm from outside, when* **CANDY** *appears down right with the key in her hands and moves towards the chair. The horn continues to beep.)* Sorry about that, hit the wrong button. *(She holds up the key.* **TRACI** *stands, grabs the key and clicks it off and the beeping stops.)* Pretty sure I'll get it right this time. *(Exits down right.)*

TRACI. I certainly hope so.

BEATRICE. Traci, how do you know he's not marrying you for your money and social position?

TRACI. Mother, Peter doesn't care about money and social position.

BEATRICE. Again, you make my point for me. If he had to go through all the trouble of becoming a lawyer, why couldn't he have picked an area of law where he could make a lot of money.

TRACI. Mother, it seems to me that most lawyers today seem to care more and more about the money in their pockets, and less and less about true justice. I'm proud of Peter.

BEATRICE. If only he was a doctor.

TRACI. Mother, a few months ago you were pushing the lawyers from your country club at me.

BEATRICE. That's different.

TRACI. Why is that different?

BEATRICE. Because – it just is. I do wish that girl would hurry up with the bags, I would like to rest and freshen up. I want to look my best for our meeting with Madame Coco.

CANDY. *(Enters from down right pulling two small suitcases on wheels. She has another bag with a strap around her neck. On her head she is wearing a big floppy hat, with the keys dangling from her mouth. She moves left a few steps as* **BEATRICE** *stands and crosses right with her purse.* **CANDY** *leans forward, indicating she wants* **BEATRICE** *to take the keys.* **BEATRICE** *rolls her eyes and with the very tips of her thumb and forefinger,*

takes the keys and carefully drops them into her purse.)
Okay, here we go, I think I got it all.

BEATRICE. Just a moment. (**CANDY** *drops the two bags.)*
Before we go to our rooms, I would like to confirm our
appointment time with Madame Coco. We had a long
discussion on the phone, and the detailed plan and
summary she e-mailed us was phenomenal.

CANDY. *(Takes the bag off her neck, sets it down, then
hands the hat to* **BEATRICE**.*)* She's the best. I'll go get
Ms. Brown, she takes care of the scheduling with
Madame Coco. *(She moves up stage to the kitchen
and opens the door.)* Audrina, the Smythes (**BEATRICE**
reacts.) are here and want to talk with you. *(She moves
back down stage to the luggage followed by* **AUDRINA**
who moves down stage.)

AUDRINA. Good morning, welcome to the Lovers' Landing
Beach Hotel. (**BEATRICE** *and* **TRACI** *stand.)* My name is
Audrina Brown, how may I help you?

BEATRICE. Hello, I'm Beatrice Rutherford-Smythe and this
is my daughter Traci. We're here for the weekend to
discuss a destination wedding with Madame Coco. We
were told we'd be able to meet with her this morning,
and just wondered where and at what time?

TRACI. I can't wait to meet her. When we spoke on the
phone she had so many wonderful ideas.

AUDRINA. Well, she usually likes to meet people here in the
lobby, and as to the time I should tell you, that Madame
Coco, like so many brilliant artistic people, marches to
her own drummer. Why don't you get settled in while
I get a hold of her and then I can confirm the time.
Candy, would you please show the Rutherford-Smythes
to their rooms and then run down to Madame Coco's
villa and find out what time she's available to meet with
them. If any one else checks in I'll handle it. Thanks.

BEATRICE. Excellent, come along Traci. (**CANDY** *picks up the
two suitcases leaving the bag on the floor.* **BEATRICE** *and
TRACI *stop and look at* **CANDY**, *look at the bag, and back
again at* **CANDY**, *who puts the two suitcases down, picks*

up the bag and puts it around her neck, then picks up the two suitcases and exits up left, followed by **BEATRICE** *and* **TRACI**.*)*

AUDRINA. *(Picks up the rum punch glasses and walks up stage as* **DOUGLAS DUPONT** *enters from down right. He has a small carry-on wheeled bag. He is dressed in shorts, a polo shirt, and sandals.* **AUDRINA** *sees him and turns to greet him, putting the glasses on the counter.)* Hello, welcome to Lovers' Landing Beach Hotel, home of sandy toes and salty kisses. I'm Audrina Brown, how may I help you?

DOUGLAS. Hi, I'm Doug DuPont. I have a reservation.

AUDRINA. *(Moving behind the counter checking the computer.)* Great, let's get you checked in so you can enjoy our beautiful beach. Ah, here you are in room twenty-two.

DOUGLAS. Oh, I guess that's alright, but I was here six months ago and just fell in love with room seven. Might it be available?

AUDRINA. Let me check. Well, you're in luck. It's been assigned to a Mr. Mudd, but as he hasn't arrived yet, I'll just put him in room twenty-two and you can have room number seven. Just fill in this card please. *(She hands him a card and a pen.)*

DOUGLAS. That's terrific, thank you. I don't remember seeing you the last time I was here. I remember meeting a Mr. Archie Brown. I believe he's the owner. Are you related?

AUDRINA. Yes, he was my father, but he passed away a few weeks ago. I'm the new owner now.

DOUGLAS. I'm very sorry for your loss. He seemed like a very nice gentleman. Please accept my condolences.

AUDRINA. Thank you. So, you were here before. If you don't mind my asking, what brings you back?

DOUGLAS. Beautiful beaches, fun times. Does there have to be a reason?

AUDRINA. No, of course not. It's just that most of our guests these days are here for destination weddings. I was just wondering if –

DOUGLAS. *(Laughing.)* I can assure you that I am not here for a wedding and definitely not mine.

AUDRINA. Ah, but it's the home of sandy toes and salty kisses. So beware the mystique of Lovers' Landing Beach Hotel.

DOUGLAS. Do you really believe in that? *(Hands her the card.)*

AUDRINA. All I can tell you is this place seems to have a magical effect on people.

DOUGLAS. Thanks, I'll remember that. Oh, do you still have that bingo game going on?

AUDRINA. Every Tuesday night. Now, please, feel free to help yourself to our complimentary drinks. I hope you'll enjoy your stay with us. Room seven is such a lovely room, and with direct access to the beach I can see why you liked it. If there's anything else you need please let me know. *(She hands him the key.)*

DOUGLAS. Thanks. I hope I'll see you later. *(He takes his bag, crosses left and exits into room 7.)*

BUBBA. *(Enters from the office, now wearing a pair of baggy cargo shorts, a t-shirt that says "Macho Man," socks pulled up to his calfs and tennis shoes. He is carrying a coffee mug.)* Good morning Audrina. *(Gives her a peck on the cheek, and continues down to sit on the couch left side.)*

AUDRINA. *(Picks up a file folder from behind the counter, follows him down and sits in the chair.)* Good morning Uncle Bubba, nice shirt.

BUBBA. You like it huh? I thought it would show off my muscles. *(Does a muscle pose.)*

AUDRINA. *(Laughing.)* And how was your morning swim?

BUBBA. *(Sipping his coffee.)* Well, I reckon it was better than dancing naked through a barnyard full of hungry chickens.

AUDRINA. *(Opens the file folder.)* Speaking of chickens Uncle Bubba, what's with the turkeys?

BUBBA. Ah, so you found them huh? Oh dear.

AUDRINA. Oh dear?

BUBBA. I think I know what's coming?

AUDRINA. Well, I see on the books that we buy twenty turkeys every week, yet we have nothing on our dining room menu made out of turkey. Why are we buying them and what do we do with them?

BUBBA. Okay, you know the huge barn like building at the back of the property.

AUDRINA. Of course, it's the original old Lovers' Landing, I used to play in it all the time when I was a little girl. Are you avoiding answering my question?

BUBBA. *(Laughing.)* I always did think you asked too many questions. Give me a second and I'll explain. You see, I've always been in charge of the entertainment in the hotel. As you know, for years every Tuesday evening we hold a bingo game for our guests and the locals. It's become very popular, so now I hold it in that old building. What you might not know, is that it's illegal to have cash prizes for bingo games in this state. So, I use turkeys.

AUDRINA. That's very creative Uncle Bubba. However, the money from the bingo games, other than the cost of the turkeys, doesn't seem to appear anywhere in the books. Why?

BUBBA. Because it's too profitable, that's why.

AUDRINA. Profitable? But that's a good thing.

BUBBA. Yes and no. On average about two-hundred people show up for bingo. We ask for a ten dollar donation per card, per game. There are twenty games, which means we take in roughly forty-thousand dollars.

AUDRINA. Forty-thousand dollars? *(Frowning.)* Wait a minute, why in heaven's name would anyone in their right mind pay ten dollars for a one in two hundred chance to win a turkey?

BUBBA. Well, it's not so much the turkey as it is the stuffing.

AUDRINA. I'm not following you.

BUBBA. The stuffing is actually ten one-hundred dollar bills.

AUDRINA. But you just said that's illegal.

BUBBA. Maybe, maybe not. As far as the local sheriff is concerned, he doesn't care what the turkeys are stuffed with as long as we keep giving away turkeys.

AUDRINA. The sheriff knows about this?

BUBBA. You betcha, his mother won three times last year.

AUDRINA. And this "donation" does not appear on the profit and loss statements?

BUBBA. Why would it? It's a...

BUBBA.   ⎱ "donation."
AUDRINA. ⎰ "donation."

> (**CANDY** *enters from down right and crosses left.*)

AUDRINA. So Candy, did you talk with Madame Coco?

CANDY. No, she wasn't around, but she left this note with your name on it. *(Hands the note to **AUDRINA** who silently reads it.)* Oh, I almost forgot. *(She reaches into her bra and pulls out several pieces of paper, which she hands to **BUBBA**.)* Your messages this morning.

BUBBA. Thanks. *(He puts the papers in his pocket then turns to **AUDRINA**.)* Well what does it say?

AUDRINA. *(Moves to the couch right and hands him the letter.)* She's eloped.

BUBBA. ⎱ What?
CANDY. ⎰ What?

AUDRINA. She says she's sorry, but when he asked, she couldn't say no. She's in love.

CANDY. That's so romantic. *(She perches on the arm of the chair.)*

BUBBA. Wedding planners don't elope.

AUDRINA. Well this one did. Oh no, what are we going to do? The Rutherford-Smythes are waiting to meet with

Madame Coco. Uncle Bubba, do you know of anyone who could possibly fill in for her this weekend?

BUBBA. Nope.

CANDY. I don't think that Rutherford-Smythes are going to settle for anyone but Madame Coco.

AUDRINA. I agree. What are we going to do? *(Pauses.)* Hold it, I'm about to be brilliant. They've never actually seen her, so what we need is someone who can impersonate her, someone who knows all about the wedding arrangements here at the hotel.

CANDY. Don't look at me. I've only worked here two weeks, and besides I've already met them.

AUDRINA. Well I can't do it either, they've already met me.

(**AUDRINA** *and* **CANDY** *both look at* **BUBBA.**)

BUBBA. Don't even think about it. (**AUDRINA** *and* **CANDY** *just look at him.*) NO!

AUDRINA. You're the only one who's worked with Madame Coco, no one else knows what she comes up with for weddings.

BUBBA. What is it you don't understand? The N or the O?

AUDRINA. Mrs. Rutherford-Smythe wants to book the entire hotel for three nights. Do you know how much money that is?

BUBBA. Of course I do, but it will never work, we'd never get away with it.

CANDY. Forgive me Mr. Brown, but I think you'd make a terrific Madame Coco.

BUBBA. This is ridiculous, what would I wear?

AUDRINA. Well, Madame Coco wasn't exactly petite, so let's go down to her villa and see what we can come up with. *(She almost pulls* **BUBBA** *up off the couch, and drags him down left.)*

BUBBA. This is insane. *(Protesting all the way.)* This has got to be the stupidest thing I've ever done in my entire life. She's never going to believe I'm a woman. Why is this happening to me?

AUDRINA. Oh, I forgot, I should check Madame Coco's schedule for the rest of the day. Candy, be an angel and go with Uncle Bubba and help him find something to wear.

BUBBA. Audrina, what did I ever do to you?

AUDRINA. I love you Uncle Bubba, you're the best. (**AUDRINA** *gives him a kiss on the cheek and then a little push towards the down left exit followed by* **CANDY**.)

> (*Enter* **PETER MUDD** *from down right. He is wearing a sports coat, collared shirt (no tie), pants and loafers. He has a small overnight bag. He moves upstage to the desk and rings the bell.*)

(*Still watching* **BUBBA** *leave, is startled.*) Oh, hello, I didn't hear you come in. (*Moves to behind the reservation counter.*) Welcome to Lovers' Landing Beach Hotel, I'm the owner Audrina Brown. How may I help you?

PETER. Hi, I'm Peter Mudd. I believe I have a reservation.

AUDRINA. You're the Rutherford-Smythe fiancé. Congratulations, you must be very excited about the big day.

PETER. Thank you. I'm a little nervous as well. Is Traci here?

AUDRINA. Yes, she checked in with her mother a little while ago.

PETER. Right, the dragon lady.

AUDRINA. That's what you call your future mother-in-law?

PETER. Not to her face, I value my life.

AUDRINA. Well, I must admit that Mrs. Rutherford-Smythe appears to be a bit daunting at times, but I'm sure she must like you. After all, you are marrying her daughter.

PETER. Do you know she actually tried to bribe me not to marry Traci?

AUDRINA. Oh dear, I can see why you'd be a little nervous then. Well, I'm sure everything is going to be just fine. If you want, I can get you a barracuda.

PETER. That would be great, but how would I get it into her bathtub?

AUDRINA. No, no, a barracuda is our rum punch drink. We call them that because they've got quite a bite.

PETER. So does she.

AUDRINA. I'm sure she has a special place in her heart for you.

PETER. Sure she does, somewhere between an IRS auditor and hemorrhoids.

AUDRINA. It can't be all that bad.

PETER. You don't think so? If I was drowning, she'd be the first person to hold out an electric cattle prod.

AUDRINA. *(Laughing.)* Okay, well let's get you checked in. If you'll just sign this. *(Hands* **PETER** *a card to sign. She takes the card and hands him the room key.)* You'll be in room twenty-two. It's just down that hallway. Do you need some help with your luggage?

PETER. No thanks, I've got it. I just want to go and change before I meet my beautiful bride-to-be. *(Exits up left with his luggage.)*

AUDRINA. *(Looks at the computer.)* This is good, the only appointment Madame Coco has today is the Rutherford-Smythes. *(***CANDY** *enters from down left in a hurry.)* How's it going with Madame Coco? Any luck with finding something to fit?

CANDY. We found clothes and a wig, but there's no way any of the shoes will work. I have to be honest, that is one ugly looking Madame Coco. He's not a happy camper and I really don't know if he's going to go through with this.

AUDRINA. Don't worry, I'll talk to him. Let's just hope Uncle Bubba can pull this off. Please tell Mrs. Rutherford-Smythe and her daughter that Madame Coco will meet them here, in the lobby, in about five minutes. *(Turns to leave, then turns back.)* Oh, and if you can get them to drink another barracuda, it couldn't hurt. *(Exits down left.)*

CANDY. *(Moves to the counter and picks up the phone as* **BEATRICE** *enters from up left carrying an envelope.)* Gee are you clairvoyant? I was just about to call you. Madame Coco can meet with you here in about five minutes.

BEATRICE. That's wonderful. Are you alone?

CANDY. *(Looks around.)* No, I'm here with you.

BEATRICE. *(Moves to the couch and sits right.)* Come and sit down please. I have a little proposal I would like to make to you. (**CANDY** *sits in the chair.)* I heard you mention earlier, that you were hoping to go to college.

CANDY. Yes Ma'am, I don't want to be a receptionist for the rest of my life. Just as soon as I've saved up enough money, I'm out of here and back to school.

BEATRICE. It is important to have goals. Maybe I can help. How would you like to earn a quick thousand dollars this weekend?

CANDY. A thousand dollars? Wow, that's a lot of money. What would I have to do?

BEATRICE. Well, it is no secret that I strongly disapprove of my daughter's choice of husband. They hardly know each other, and I'm afraid he's marrying her for her money and social position. Although I've only known him for a short time, I'm afraid he can't be trusted.

CANDY. What does all that have to do with me?

BEATRICE. I'm getting to that. I simply want you to flirt with him.

CANDY. *(Pauses.)* Define flirt.

BEATRICE. You know, come on to him just a little bit and then report back to me what his reaction was.

CANDY. *(Pauses.)* Define a little bit.

BEATRICE. Well, I'm certainly not asking you to do anything that you wouldn't be comfortable doing. What I want to know is what his reaction will be, when, a short while before he is to be married, a pretty girl makes a pass at him.

CANDY. I guess I could do that. As long as that's all I have to do and no one gets hurt.

BEATRICE. Thank you. I really am worried about my daughter. *(She hands the envelope to* **CANDY**.*)*

CANDY. Okay. It sounds harmless enough and I sure could use the thousand dollars.

BEATRICE. Terrific. Remember he'll be in room seven. *(She stands and moves upstage left.)* I'll tell Traci about the meeting. *(Exits up left.)*

CANDY. *(Stands and heads towards the office.)* A thousand dollars just to flirt? That woman must have more money than sense. Wow! *(She kisses the envelope as the land line phone rings. She hurries behind the counter, puts the envelope down and picks up the phone.)* Lovers' Landing Beach Hotel, home of sandy toes and salty kisses. *(***DOUGLAS**, *now wearing swim trunks, a swim shirt and flip flops, opens the door of room seven. He has a cell phone in his hand. He is about to step into the room when, just visible to the audience and unnoticed by* **CANDY**, *he stops to listen.)* I'm sorry Charley that's not possible, you know the rules, you call on the land line, I take your name and number and Pegasus calls you back. *(Writing on a piece of paper.)* Okay, got it. Thank you. *(She hangs up and puts a slip of paper down the front of her bra, as* **DOUGLAS** *records a note on his phone then steps into the room, closing the door behind him.)* Well, hi there.

DOUGLAS. Hello.

CANDY. I'm Candy, I didn't realize you had checked in.

DOUGLAS. You know who I am?

CANDY. Oh sure, I'm the receptionist here. Audrina must have checked you in.

DOUGLAS. She did. She seems very nice.

CANDY. She is. Can I help you with anything?

DOUGLAS. No, I'm good. Thank you.

CANDY. Okay, if you do, just ring the bell. *(Picks up the envelope and exits to the kitchen.)*

DOUGLAS. *(Looks around and crosses quickly right to the sign and takes a photograph with his phone. He then moves to the left of the drinks table as* **CANDY** *re-enters from the office unseen by* **DOUGLAS** *as he takes another photograph of the drinks table. She quickly fluffs her hair, and hitches up her bra. She comes up behind him and taps him on the shoulder, takes a step or two back and tries to strike a sexy pose.)*
(Turns and sees her.) Oh hello again.

CANDY. *(In a sexy voice.)* Hi there.

DOUGLAS. Is there something I can do for you?

CANDY. I hope not.

DOUGLAS. What?

CANDY. What I mean is – I'm not sure what I mean.

DOUGLAS. *(Moves left towards her.)* Why don't you tell me what this is all about?

CANDY. Oh dear, I knew I wouldn't be very good at this. Okay, here goes. *(She raises her skirt a little, shows some leg and licks her lips.)* What would you do if I tried to kiss you?

DOUGLAS. Well this is a first. I've never been approached quite like that before. Well now, what would any red-blooded American male do?

CANDY. I don't know.

DOUGLAS. I'd probably kiss you back.

CANDY. Oh dear, this is getting out of hand. You wouldn't really would you?

DOUGLAS. Why not?

CANDY. Because you're not supposed to.

DOUGLAS. Why not? I can't think of anything I'd rather be doing than kissing a beautiful girl right now.

CANDY. Oh dear.

DOUGLAS. So, are you going to kiss me?

CANDY. No.

DOUGLAS. Why not?

CANDY. Well, since we've established that you would kiss me back, then we don't actually have to do it.

DOUGLAS. You know, you may be cute, but you're not making a whole lot of sense. Tell you what, would you like to meet me later for champagne and watch the sunset from the beach? *(The phone on the counter rings.)*

CANDY. You're not supposed to say things like that.

DOUGLAS. Why not? It's a terrific way to get to know each other. *(The phone rings again.)* Don't you need to get that?

CANDY. Ah, right. *(Moves behind the counter and picks up the phone.)* Hello, Lovers' Landing Beach... Oh, hi Audrina. *(Pauses.)* Yes, I told them and they said they'd be right out. *(Clicks off the phone.)* Why did you take a photograph of a pitcher of rum punch?

DOUGLAS. What?

CANDY. The rum punch. Most people drink theirs. How come you took a picture of it instead.

DOUGLAS. What? Oh, well, I guess that would seem a little strange wouldn't it?

CANDY. You reckon?

DOUGLAS. Listen Candy, I'm just not at liberty to answer that question.

CANDY. Oh – oh – oh, that sounds like something James Bond would say. Is it because you're some type of agent?

DOUGLAS. Something like that.

CANDY. You mean you're a spy?

DOUGLAS. *(Laughs.)* No, nothing like that.

CANDY. Oh, that's a shame. I've always wanted to meet a spy. Ah well, is there anything else you need right now?

DOUGLAS. I guess not, unless you change your mind about that kiss.

CANDY. I don't think I should.

DOUGLAS. Well you never know. If you do, the invitation still holds, champagne on the beach at sunset. *(Exits down left.)*

CANDY. Oh my, this isn't good. *(Exits to the office.)*

> *(**BEATRICE** enters from upstage left with her purse which contains a wedding brochure and letter, followed by **TRACI**, minus the scarf. **BEATRICE** looks around and seeing no-one marches to the counter, followed by **TRACI** who stands to her left. **BEATRICE** rings the bell once. She pauses and then rings the bell a second time.)*

BEATRICE. You see Traci why this place is unacceptable, there's never anyone here to be of service. *(**BEATRICE** is now furiously ringing the bell as **CANDY** enters from the office on the run, grabs the bell from her and returns to the office with the bell.)* Well, I never. There, you see Traci –

TRACI. Mother, please don't start up again. We're here, I'm marrying Peter and that's that.

BEATRICE. Well if you have to marry him, does it have to be here?

> *(**CANDY** enters from the office with the bell and a paper placard that says "RING ONCE" which she places on the counter in front of **BEATRICE**. She then moves a step or two right ignoring **BEATRICE** and appears to be busy at the computer. **BEATRICE** pauses, looks at the sign, then at **CANDY**, and finally rings the bell once.)*

CANDY. *(Turns with a huge smile on her face.)* Can I help you?

BEATRICE. I thought we were meeting Madame Coco. *(Looks at her watch.)* She appears to be late.

CANDY. I'm sure she'll be here soon.

TRACI. I'm so excited, I can't wait to see her.

> *(**AUDRINA** enters from down left holding "MADAME COCO" by the hand and almost pulling her into the room. **CANDY** covers her*

mouth with her hand to suppress a laugh. **BUBBA** *is now totally transformed. He is wearing an ankle length, summer flowered dress, a blonde long curly haired wig, a very large straw sun hat, and a large pair of flamboyant sunglasses. He is barefoot and has ample "bosoms."* **AUDRINA** *and* **MADAME COCO** *cross towards the counter.) [SEE AUTHORS' NOTES.]*

AUDRINA. Mrs. Rutherford-Smythe, may I present Madame Coco.

BEATRICE. I'm so thrilled to finally meet you in person.

BUBBA. The pleasure is all mine. *(They shake hands.)*

BEATRICE. This is my daughter, Traci.

TRACI. Hello. *(They shake hands.)*

BUBBA. Such a beautiful bride.

AUDRINA. Shall we sit down?

BUBBA. *(Aside to* **CANDY** *not heard by* **BEATRICE** *and* **TRACI**.*)* Candy, get me out of this! **(CANDY** *exits to the office still trying not to laugh.)*

> *(***BEATRICE** *sits on the couch left and* **TRACI** *sits on the couch right. She is taking out the brochure and letter as* **BUBBA** *goes to sit in the chair.* **BUBBA** *hitches his dress up and sits with his knees wide apart.* **AUDRINA**, *not noticed by* **BEATRICE** *or* **TRACI**, *quickly pushes his knees together, pulls down the dress and perches on the left arm of the chair.)*

BEATRICE. Traci and I are delighted to meet you. We've read the brochure you sent us and loved the wonderful ideas you had to make my daughter's wedding day so special. How ever did you come up with rose petals floating down from the ceiling of the wedding chapel?

BUBBA. Well, I just imagine the scene. It takes the genius of Mr. Brown to actually make it happen. **(AUDRINA** *glares* *at him.)* Without him and his technical ability it would be just another wedding.

BEATRICE. He must be an amazing man.

BUBBA. Well, I'm not sure amazing is quite the right word, but – on second thought, maybe it is the right word.

AUDRINA. Perhaps we should move on from the Mr. Brown admiration society. I believe you said you had some questions.

BEATRICE. Just one or two minor things. First, how does the wedding party get from the hotel to the chapel?

BUBBA. They walk.

TRACI. What mother means is will there be a runner?

BUBBA. Who's running where?

AUDRINA. What Madame Coco means is that because this is the home of sandy toes and salty kisses, the bridal party and their guests go barefoot to the wedding. It creates the feeling of oneness with nature.

BEATRICE. But I was planning on wearing my Prada shoes. Rutherford-Smythes do not go barefoot.

BUBBA. Why not? Is there something wrong with your feet?

AUDRINA. What Madame Coco means is that everyone loves the feeling of sand between their toes on the wedding day, and you wouldn't want to miss this special opportunity. It really creates an aura of simplicity and intimacy. Why it's been a tradition at Lovers' Landing forever.

TRACI. Mother, it sounds delightful, and it's what I want. You can wear your shoes for the reception.

BEATRICE. What do we do if it rains?

BUBBA. You get wet.

AUDRINA. Of course you would if you were outside. *(Glares at* **BUBBA.***)* But, it very rarely rains here at this time of year, and we have a fabulous old barn that can hold hundreds of people. It's where you will be having the reception, and it would be no trouble at all to hold the wedding there as well, if the weather was bad.

TRACI. See mother, I told you this was a perfect location.

BEATRICE. *(With total disdain.)* A barn?

AUDRINA. *(Mimicking the way* **BEATRICE** *pronounced barn.)* Well, it's not really a barn, it was originally built during the civil war. The building is rustic...

BEATRICE. Rustic?

AUDRINA. In a fashionable way of course, especially when it is decorated with hundreds of tiny twinkling lights. It was the original landing where the Confederate Army would bring in horses from Mexico. It's located on the intracoastal side of the property, and it's a National Historic Landmark.

BEATRICE. Really? That is impressive.

AUDRINA. Tell you what, after our meeting is over, I'll ask Mr. Brown to take you over there and give you a tour. I'm sure he'd be happy to do that. *(***BUBBA** *gives* **AUDRINA** *a "look.")*

CANDY. *(Enters from the office.)* Excuse me please, but there's a phone call for Madame Coco.

AUDRINA. Would you please just take a message Candy.

CANDY. Er, er, they said it was urgent.

BUBBA. Right. *(Stands.)* Ladies please excuse me. *(Moves quickly up stage and exits to the office followed by* **CANDY**.*)*

AUDRINA. I'm so sorry for the interruption. As I mentioned earlier, Madame Coco is um...ah, unpredictable.

BEATRICE. Will she return?

AUDRINA. I certainly hope so.

BEATRICE. Well, it's quite obvious she's in high demand. So, you hold the wedding reception in a National Historic Landmark building. I believe that would be a first even for the Rutherford-Smythes.

TRACI. Mother, let's not go down that road.

BEATRICE. *(Doesn't miss a beat.)* I don't believe the Cabot-Lodges have ever had a reception in a National Historic Landmark building.

TRACI. Down the road we go.

BEATRICE. Traci, if you insist on marrying Peter Mudd, at least it will be in a prestigious place. That's something to be thankful for.

TRACI. Mother –

BUBBA. *(Now dressed as himself, in baggy cargo shorts and Macho Man t-shirt, calf length socks and tennis shoes. He enters from the office and comes down stage.* **AUDRINA** *stands and looks daggers at him.)* Audrina my dear, please introduce me to these lovely ladies.

AUDRINA. What?

BUBBA. *(Moves left, steps across in front of* **AUDRINA,** *and offers his hand first to* **BEATRICE** *then to* **TRACI.)** Ladies, allow me to introduce myself. I am Audrina's uncle, Wilberforce Brown. *(He makes his best effort to bow and they shake hands.)*

AUDRINA. Wilberforce?

BEATRICE. I'm sure I speak for both of us when I say we are delighted to meet you Wilberforce.

BUBBA. The feeling is mutual. Audrina why don't you sit down. *(***AUDRINA** *sits in the chair and* **BUBBA** *remains standing above* **AUDRINA***'s chair.)* Madame Coco sends her apologies. In the meantime, is there anything I can help you with?

BEATRICE. Ms. Brown suggested that you would be able to show us the building for the reception.

BUBBA. The pleasure would be all mine.

BEATRICE. Excellent. There is however one more question.

BUBBA. Yes?

BEATRICE. Well, er – it's a question I'd be more comfortable asking Madame Coco.

AUDRINA. *(Standing.)* We understand perfectly. Uncle Bu –
  Wilberforce, why don't you go and see if Madame Coco
  has finished her phone call.

BUBBA. *(Gives* **AUDRINA** *"a look.")* Well, she did say she may
  be tied up for quite awhile. *(He pauses as* **AUDRINA**
  simply nods her head for him to go.) I'll go, but only as
  a favor to these lovely ladies. *(Exits to the office.)*

BEATRICE. What a charming man. Is he married?

TRACI. Mother!

AUDRINA. No, the mystique of Lovers' Landing has alluded
  him so far.

BEATRICE. My, what a shame.

TRACI. Mom, you're looking quite flushed.

BEATRICE. I most certainly am not. Rutherford-Smythes do
  not get flushed.

TRACI. It's okay, I'm just teasing you.

BEATRICE. Oh, I see. But I am not flushed. *(Fanning herself.)*
  It's just a little warm in here.

TRACI. Me thinks thou doth protest too much.

> *(Enter* **BUBBA**, *now dressed as* **MADAME COCO**,
> *from the office.)* [SEE AUTHORS' NOTES.]

AUDRINA. Ah, Madame Coco, welcome back. *(Stands and
  indicates that* **BUBBA** *should sit in the chair. He is about
  to sit, as he did previously with knees wide apart, when
  he sees* **AUDRINA** *glaring at him and quickly recovers to
  sit ever so daintily, his knees together and to one side.*
  AUDRINA *smiles her approval, and again perches on the
  left arm.)* Now Mrs. Rutherford-Smythe, I believe you
  have another question for us.

BEATRICE. Well, it's a small thing really, and I'm sure you're
  asked it all the time, but I was wondering, when we're
  out on the beach, where do we go if we need the little
  girls' room?

BUBBA. The little girls' room?

AUDRINA. What Madame Coco means is when you're at the wedding chapel, the nearest bathroom is quite accessible, isn't it Madame Coco?

BUBBA. Um, right. *(Now getting into the role.)* Right, I do know how important it is for us girls to be close to the little girls' room. It always seems as if you have to wait in line forever and sometimes it feels like you're never going to make it in time. I...

AUDRINA. Thank you Madame Coco. What she means is that the closest restrooms to the chapel are the pool changing rooms, and we have plenty of them. So, I'm sure there won't be any problems. Mr. Brown will be happy to show them to you if you like. (**BUBBA** *gives* **AUDRINA** *another "look."*)

TRACI. Mr. Brown appears to wear many hats around here.

BUBBA. Oh, you can say that again. He works his fingers to the bone. He's the doorman, entertainment director, receptionist and room service provider when needed, and of course the maintenance man. Why this place would have fallen into disrepair years ago if it wasn't for him.

BEATRICE. Mr. Brown seems indispensable.

BUBBA. Well I wouldn't exactly say that.

AUDRINA. *(Almost to herself.)* Yes you would, you say it all the time.

BUBBA. I do have to admit that he really is a wonderful person.

BEATRICE. It's not just that, it's his name, Wilberforce. It's so – so – masculine.

TRACI. Mother!

BUBBA. Well I'm sure she can't help herself. Mr. Brown is such a handsome man, and so gallant. Quite a catch for someone looking for an honest (**AUDRINA** *reacts.*), resourceful and extremely talented executive. Don't you think so Audrina?

AUDRINA. I believe you forgot the word modest. However I do agree, uncle Bu – Wilberforce is quite a character.

BEATRICE. I look forward to him showing me, um, I mean us around. Madame Coco, will you be available later? I'm sure after our tour we will have a few more questions.

AUDRINA. I can assure you that Madame Coco will be here, if you need her.

TRACI. It has been a pleasure meeting with you Madame Coco. I'm so excited about having the wedding here.

CANDY. *(Enters from the office on the run.)* Sorry to butt in Audrina, but I just looked out the office window and the parking lot is beginning to flood. It looks like a sprinkler head has broken.

BUBBA. *(Stands.)* What?

AUDRINA. Oh dear, Madame Coco, would you mind finding Uncle Bubba, he might be somewhere near the office. Candy, look to see if he's in the kitchen. I'll go and check outside. Please excuse us. *(Rushes out the front door.)*

> (**BUBBA** *quickly exits to the office and* **CANDY** *rushes to the kitchen.)*

BEATRICE. My Mercedes! Traci, quick *(Gets the keys out of her purse.)* We need to move the car before it gets wet.

TRACI. But mother...

BEATRICE. Now Traci, I can't afford for anything to happen to that car.

TRACI. But I might get my feet wet.

BEATRICE. Make the sacrifice. Better your feet than my Mercedes.

TRACI. But mother...

BEATRICE. Now Tracy. *(Hands her the keys and* **TRACI** *moves quickly right.)*

> *(Enter* **BUBBA** *from the office on a dead run without socks or shoes. He exits the front door followed by* **CANDY** *from the kitchen who is carrying a bucket and a mop on her right shoulder. As she moves down stage from the kitchen she is in* **TRACI***'s way. As* **TRACI***, tries*

to step around her left side **CANDY** *whips around when she hears* **BEATRICE** *call her.)*

Candy.

CANDY. Yes? *(It looks for a moment as though* **TRACI** *is going to get hit by the mop, but without missing a stride* **TRACI** *ducks under it and continues out the front door.)* [SEE AUTHORS' NOTES.]

BEATRICE. Good, we're alone. Has Mr. Mudd checked in yet? I haven't seen him.

CANDY. *(Setting down the bucket and mop.)* Oh, he's here alright.

BEATRICE. And?

CANDY. *(Moves left to sit on the couch right side.)* I don't think you're going to like it.

BEATRICE. *(Leaning forward.)* Tell me about it.

CANDY. Well, I did what you told me, then he said there wasn't anything he'd rather be doing than kissing me, *(**BEATRICE** reacts.)* and then he invited me to meet him later for champagne at sunset on the beach.

BEATRICE. *(Stands, pumps a fist, claps her hands and gives* **CANDY** *two thumbs up.)* Right, I just knew he was up to no good. *(Opens her purse.)* Well done Candy, here's a little bonus. *(Holds out a $100 bill.)*

CANDY. *(Puts her hands up.)* No, please, I just don't feel right about any of this. I don't want anyone to get hurt.

BEATRICE. Traci will be fine, but I can't speak for Peter. The cad!

CANDY. Well, I'm glad I don't have to do that again. I hope it all works out for you Mrs. Smythe.

BEATRICE. That's Rutherford-Smythe. *(**CANDY** picks up the bucket and mop, and heads towards the front entrance.)*

*(**TRACI** enters through the front entrance, and narrowly misses being hit again by the mop as* **CANDY** *exits.)*

Traci dear, come sit here, I have something I need to tell you.

TRACI. *(Moves left and sits on the couch right side.)* In case you're wondering, your Mercedes is just fine.

BEATRICE. That's nice. Traci, Peter is here. *(**TRACI** stands as if to go find him, but she pulls her back down.)* You need to be sitting down when I tell you this. I'm afraid Traci, that Peter is proving himself to be unworthy of marrying you.

TRACI. Mother, I am not going to sit here and listen to you malign Peter again, and stop smiling. You look like the Mona Lisa on valium.

BEATRICE. I wish I wasn't the bearer of this news, as I know it's going to hurt you, but I'm just trying to protect you from making a terrible decision. Please listen to me. I just found out from Candy, the receptionist, that Peter was coming on to her.

TRACI. That's a lie.

BEATRICE. She er – ran into him and one thing led to another and he told her there was nothing he'd rather be doing than kissing her. He then went on to invite her to meet him later at sunset for champagne on the beach.

TRACI. Are you sure? *(**BEATRICE** nods affirmatively.)* *(**TRACI** stands.)* I'm going to kill him! He's going to regret the day he was born! *(Storms to the door of room 7, shakes the door handle trying to get in, then hammers on the door.)* Peter Mudd, get your miserable, lying, cheating, two timing, philandering slimy self out of there.

BEATRICE. *(Moves up to her.)* Traci dear, don't you think –

TRACI. *(Still yelling through the door.)* Sooner or later you're going to have to come out, and I'll be waiting for you. *(Ignoring **BEATRICE**, she storms off down left.)*

BEATRICE. Traci, I really think you're over-reacting, please – *(Follows her off down left.)*

BUBBA. *(Enters from down right, followed by **CANDY**, still carrying the bucket and mop, and **AUDRINA**.)* Girl, what do you think you were going to do with a bucket and mop in the parking lot?

CANDY. Clean up the water of course.

AUDRINA. Candy, we appreciate your trying to help out. Now, why don't you go put that away. (**CANDY** *exits to the kitchen.*) Uncle Bubba, thank you, *(Gives him a kiss on the cheek.)* you saved the day again.

BUBBA. That's my job. By the way, did you enjoy my performance as Madame Coco?

AUDRINA. Uncle Bubba, I love you, but on a scale of one to ten – NO. *(She looks around.)* I wonder where Traci and her mother went.

BUBBA. I don't care as long as I don't have to wear that dress again.

AUDRINA. *(Moves behind the reception desk.)* Aww, but you looked so cute.

BUBBA. *(Stands with his back to up left.)* Don't start with me Audrina, I've had a very rough day so far.

AUDRINA. *(Laughing.)* Yes Wilberforce.

BUBBA. Well…that's my name isn't it?

AUDRINA. There's nothing to be embarrassed about, she seemed to be very impressed with you, *(Starts to giggle.)* both of you actually. It was quite apparent that the two of you have made a connection.

> (**BEATRICE** *enters from up left, minus the blazer, and carrying a floppy hat. She overhears* **BUBBA**.)

BUBBA. Well, I must admit, I did find her rather attractive.

BEATRICE. *(Crosses to* **BUBBA**.*)* Why thank you Wilberforce. Now, didn't I hear you say I was going to get a personal tour of the property?

AUDRINA. You most certainly did. Right Uncle Bubba?

BUBBA. Right, will your daughter be joining us?

BEATRICE. No she won't. She's a little distracted at the moment.

BUBBA. Well then, *(Gallantly takes* **BEATRICE**'s *arm and leads her towards the front door.)* let the tour begin.

(**BUBBA** *and* **BEATRICE** *stop by the sign and he points towards the "shoes."* **BEATRICE** *looks at the sign, then him, then shakes her head "no."* **BUBBA**, *folds his arms, smiles and nods his head slowly, "yes."* **BEATRICE**, *looks at him, pauses for a second or two, then giggles, takes her shoes off and puts them in the tray. She puts her hat on, takes his arm and they exit down left as* **CANDY** *enters from the kitchen.*)

AUDRINA. I think the magic of sandy toes and salty kisses has finally gotten to Uncle Bubba.

CANDY. With who?

AUDRINA. Mrs. Rutherford-Smythe.

CANDY. Oh dear.

AUDRINA. Oh dear?

DOUGLAS. *(Enters from room 7.)* Hi gorgeous.

CANDY.
AUDRINA. } Hi. *(They immediately look at each other.)*

DOUGLAS. I think you should know there's a crazy lady out there on the beach yelling and throwing coconuts around. I nearly got clobbered by one.

AUDRINA. Candy, quick go check it out and see what's going on and then get back to me. (**CANDY** *quickly rushes into the kitchen.*) You're going the wrong way. The beach is out there.

CANDY. *(Immediately comes back out with a colander on her head.)* Better to be safe than sorry. *(Exits down left.)*

AUDRINA. Are you alright?

DOUGLAS. I'm fine.

AUDRINA. I'm really sorry about this.

DOUGLAS. Don't be, it's not your fault.

AUDRINA. It's usually so peaceful and calm on the beach. Is there anything I can get you?

DOUGLAS. No, I'm good. I've got a few phone calls to make, so I'll try the beach later when that mad woman isn't around. *(Exits to room 7, leaving the door slightly ajar.)*

> *(**CANDY** enters from down left, still wearing the colander.)*

AUDRINA. Well?

CANDY. It's the Rutherford-Smythe's daughter.

AUDRINA. And?

CANDY. Well, when I got to the beach she wasn't throwing anything, but she was yelling and screaming about her no good two timing fiancé. Oh dear. This is all my fault, and now Mr. Brown is in her clutches.

AUDRINA. How can this be your fault?

CANDY. I promised not to tell.

AUDRINA. Candy, come and sit down for a second. We need to get one or two things straightened out. *(Moves from behind the reception desk, grabs **CANDY**'s hand and they sit on the couch. **AUDRINA** left, **CANDY** right. She pauses and looks at **CANDY**.)* Are you going to wear that thing for the rest of your life? *(**CANDY** takes the colander off and sets it on the coffee table.)* Now, if you know what's going on, and it involves Uncle Bubba, don't you think you should tell me?

CANDY. *(Clearly agitated.)* Audrina, she's a home wrecker and I'm her accomplice.

AUDRINA. Who?

CANDY. The Rutherford what's it woman.

AUDRINA. Candy, you're not making any sense. Now start from the beginning.

CANDY. *(Stands and starts to pace back and forth in front of the coffee table. As she retells what happened, she talks faster and faster and becomes more and more physically dramatic re-enacting the story, and less and less verbal.)* Well, it all started when she asked me to do her a favor. Then she offered me a thousand dollars. *(Jumps around excitedly.)* I mean like wow, a thousand dollars that's so much money. All I had to do was, you know *(Bats her eyes.)*. So I went to his room and I *(Boosts up her bra.)* and then *(Hitches up her skirt and walks sexily.)* Finally I asked him to *(Kissing motions.)* Well he was like *(Turns her back, crosses her arms and hugs herself.)* and I *(Throws her hands up and shakes her head no.)* When I told her she just *(Fist pump, claps, thumbs up.)*. I know, I know, I really shouldn't have done it, but she said no one would get hurt. *(She moves back towards the couch and plops down next to **AUDRINA**.)* So, now you see why Mr. Brown is in trouble.

AUDRINA. Candy, I have no idea what you're talking about. I really don't see what this has to do with Uncle Bubba.

CANDY. Weren't you listening? Mr. Brown can't go out with that, that home wrecker. He's too nice.

AUDRINA. I'm sure it's nothing serious.

CANDY. That may be, but I know when a man starts to think with his zipper, his engine is running but there ain't nobody driving.

AUDRINA. *(Laughing.)* Candy, Uncle Bubba's a big boy and quite capable of taking care of himself.

CANDY. You know, I've been thinking, have you noticed that single women are always trying to get a husband and married women are always trying to get rid of theirs?

AUDRINA. Well, as long as it keeps us in business. Speaking of which, if I got the gist of things, it sounds like there's trouble in paradise, which doesn't bode well for a wedding.

CANDY. I'm afraid you're right about that.

AUDRINA. Hopefully it'll sort itself out. I'd better get back to the books. If you need me, I'll be in the office. *(Exits to the office.)*

CANDY. *(Picks up the colander and heads to the counter.)* I hope you're right.

> *(**TRACI** enters from down left as **CANDY** quickly ducks behind the counter. **TRACI** is now carrying a piece of driftwood with what*

*appears to be a large dead fish on it. She
marches straight towards room 7, watched
by* **CANDY** *who has put the colander on again
and peaks out from behind the counter. She
kicks the door with her foot, and it opens. She
then throws the fish into the room.)*

TRACI. You stink! *(She crosses down right still carrying the
driftwood.)* Now, for his Beemer. *(She exits down right.
Almost immediately the fish is thrown back on stage
and the door to room 7 slammed shut from the inside.)*

CANDY. *(Slowly rises from behind the counter.)* Geez, that
is one scary woman. *(She comes left from behind the
counter and looks at the fish. She bends slightly as
though to pick it up, then jerks back holding her nose.)*
I know!

> *(***CANDY*** *runs into the kitchen, there is a lot
of noise, cupboard doors, pots pans etc. and
reappears with a large oven mitt on one
hand holding a long pair of barbecue tongs
and a spray can of air freshener in the other.
She gingerly picks up the fish with the tongs,
holds it at arm's length while spraying it, and
exits down left to the beach.)*

AUDRINA. *(Enters from the office.)* Is everything all right?
What was all that noise? Candy where are you? *(***CANDY***
re-enters from down left. She is minus the fish but still
has the colander on her head the oven mitt on, carrying
the tongs like a sword and holding the spray can in
the other hand.)* Who do you think you are, Wonder
Woman?

CANDY. *(She comes up to join* **AUDRINA** *by the counter.)* We
have one angry bride to be on our hands. I think I get it
now, "Hell hath no fury like a woman scorned."

AUDRINA. I didn't realize you knew Shakespeare.

CANDY. Well, of course I never knew him, he's been dead
for five hundred years, or was it four hundred, anyways

he lived in England and I've never been there. Well, at least not in this lifetime, but who knows maybe –

AUDRINA. Candy, I didn't mean...oh never mind. Would you mind going and preparing the afternoon snack tray for our guests? I've still got work to finish up.

CANDY. You bet, I think I'll be safer in there anyways. *(Exits to the kitchen.)*

AUDRINA. Thanks. *(Exits to the office.)*

> *(TRACI enters from down right, moves up to the bar, and facing right, pours herself a drink and gulps it down as PETER, now wearing casual shorts, the same collared shirt and loafers enters from up left.)*

PETER. Traci my love. *(He stops slightly down stage from the kitchen door and puts his arms out.)*

> *(TRACI turns, sees him, marches over to him, slaps him on the face and without missing a beat continues off up left. PETER almost goes down and staggers to lean on the back wall just left of the kitchen door as CANDY comes out of the kitchen and flattens him against the wall. CANDY blissfully unaware of what she has done exits to the office as PETER slowly crumples to the floor. BEATRICE enters from down right carrying her hat followed by BUBBA They stop at the shoe tray and BUBBA picks up BEATRICE's shoes and hands them to her.)*

BUBBA. Here you are my dear.

BEATRICE. *(Takes her shoes.)* You know Wilberforce, I quite liked having sandy toes.

BUBBA. Well, you know what goes with sandy toes.

BEATRICE. You mean?

> *(They are interrupted by a groan and movement from PETER as he staggers to his feet. They break apart and BEATRICE sees PETER.)*

Excuse me Wilberforce. *(Hands her shoes and hat to* **BUBBA**, *the hat should be in his down stage hand. She marches up to* **PETER**. *She slaps him and he goes down again. She then returns to* **BUBBA**.) I am so sorry Wilberforce, but it had to be done. Now, where were we?

(**BUBBA** *takes a step towards her, takes her in his arms. He holds her shoes in his upstage hand and her hat in the other. As they kiss he slowly brings the hat up to cover their faces.)*

(Curtain.)

ACT II

(Later the same day.)

*(The curtain rises on an empty set. After a moment or two, **BUBBA** enters from down right. He is carrying a bouquet of flowers. He is dressed in his baggy cargo shorts and a collared shirt. His hair is neatly combed, he is wearing socks, pulled up, and tennis shoes. He begins to waltz around the lobby, as **CANDY** enters from the office unseen by **BUBBA**. **CANDY** stifles a laugh as **BUBBA** continues to dance with the flowers.)*

CANDY. *(Moves towards **BUBBA**.)* May I have this dance?

*(**BUBBA** simply sweeps her up and continues dancing as **AUDRINA** enters from down left. She watches them for a second or two when they finally see her and stop and break apart.)*

AUDRINA. Uncle Bubba is that you?

BUBBA. No, it's a Japanese bull fighter.

AUDRINA. What are you two doing?

BUBBA. We're imitating the mating ritual of Norwegian parrots. What does it look like we're doing? Now if you'll excuse me, I've got a delivery to make. *(Exits, still dancing, up left to the rooms.)*

CANDY. *(Moves behind the counter.)* Oh dear, poor Mr. Brown.

AUDRINA. *(Comes to the left end of the counter.)* I do believe he's been bitten by the love bug. Okay Candy, let's see what we can salvage from this morning's disaster. Have you seen Miss Traci since lunch time?

CANDY. Nope, everything's been quiet on that front, but I think we might have another problem on our hands. It's the fiancé. I caught him taking photographs of the barracudas, and at lunch time, he was taking photos of the beach bar and making notes on his phone.

AUDRINA. Why would that be a problem?

CANDY. Because, he told me he was an agent.

AUDRINA. What do you mean an agent? The Rutherford-Smythes told me he's a lawyer.

CANDY. Well, whatever he is, he seems overly interested in the drinks around here.

AUDRINA. I've got a feeling I'd better have a little talk with Uncle Bubba. *(***BUBBA*** enters from up left still holding the flowers.)* Speak of the devil. Candy, will you excuse us please.

CANDY. Sure, I'll be in the office if you need me. *(She reaches into her bra and hands* **BUBBA** *more papers, which he puts in his pocket, then exits to the office.)*

AUDRINA. Uncle Bubba, have you got a few minutes? We need to talk.

BUBBA. I'm all ears.

AUDRINA. I'd like to get your opinion on something.

BUBBA. Okay, shoot.

AUDRINA. Candy tells me the Rutherford-Smythe fiancé who checked in this morning, appears to be snooping around, photographing everything and making notes.

BUBBA. So what's wrong with that?

AUDRINA. Nothing, but what's really weird is that he told Candy he's an agent, and the Rutherford-Smythes told me he was a lawyer.

BUBBA. Are you sure about that?

AUDRINA. Of course.

BUBBA. *(Sits on the couch left and puts the flowers down on the coffee table.)* Oh boy! We may be in trouble.

AUDRINA. *(Sits in the chair.)* Why?

BUBBA. The only people I've ever heard of who employ lawyers as investigative agents are the federal government.

AUDRINA. Why would the federal government be interested in the Lovers' Landing Beach Hotel?

BUBBA. Well, not really the whole federal government, but perhaps the Bureau of Alcohol, Tobacco, Firearms and Explosives.

AUDRINA. *(Pauses and looks at him.)* Do you have something to tell me Uncle Bubba?

BUBBA. Oh dear. It's not that I wasn't going to tell you, it's just that we haven't had time and it's a bit of a long story.

AUDRINA. Make it short.

BUBBA. Well, it all started four or five years ago, when we rented the landing building to a movie company who needed it for one of their scenes. The movie was about Mexican rum being imported into the U.S. during prohibition. They set up a model of a distillery and when they were finished, rather than break it all down, they asked if I wanted it as memorabilia.

AUDRINA. This is the short version?

BUBBA. In a nutshell, I found the fermentation vats and the distilling equipment actually worked.

AUDRINA. Are you telling me that our hotel is a front for an illegal distillery?

BUBBA. Well, yes and no.

AUDRINA. What's that supposed to mean?

BUBBA. It's not illegal to distill liquor for your own use on private property. All you need is a federal fuel alcohol permit and we've got one. They don't seem to care whether you pour the alcohol down your throat or into the fuel tank of your lawnmower, as long as you don't sell it.

AUDRINA. But we do sell it.

BUBBA. Actually we don't. (**AUDRINA** *opens her mouth to protest.*) We export it.

AUDRINA. What?

BUBBA. Once a month some friends of mine from Mexico, come to the landing, and we load a couple of barrels of rum onto their fishing boat.

AUDRINA. Just how much rum is this?

BUBBA. About a hundred and ten gallons.

AUDRINA. I'm going to have a heart attack. You sell them a hundred and ten gallons a month?

BUBBA. No, that would be illegal. We give it to them.

AUDRINA. Now I'm totally confused.

BUBBA. Well, you see, they take it back to Mexico, bottle it and label it "Made in Mexico." They keep fifty percent of it, then they ship the other half back. We now pay the freight and customs duty, making the rum legal for us to sell.

AUDRINA. Uncle Bubba, you are crafty like a fox. But why would we be in trouble if it's legal?

BUBBA. Ah, in theory you can distill liquor for your own consumption, but only up to two hundred gallons a year per person. As long as you're not selling it they never check on the quantity, and if you think about it, how would they go about doing that. There's a lot of waste in the process anyway. So the quantity is a little bit of a gray area.

AUDRINA. What does your friend the sheriff say about this?

BUBBA. Nothing at all.

AUDRINA. So he doesn't know about this?

BUBBA. He does, but he gets a half gallon a month for his mother as a...

BUBBA. ⎫ gift.
AUDRINA. ⎭ gift.

AUDRINA. You know Uncle Bubba, you will never be known as the ultimate con artist.

BUBBA. Why not?

AUDRINA. You're over qualified.

BUBBA. Why thank you sweetheart I'll take that as a compliment, but I'm not at all comfortable though with this guy snooping around. Any chance you might be able to talk with him a little and see if we need to be worried?

AUDRINA. I can give it a try, I certainly don't want to see you wearing orange. It's not your color. Is there anything else I should know?

> *(Enter* **BEATRICE** *from down left, she is wearing a causal sundress, pearl earrings and is wearing sandals. Her hair is now hanging loose.)*

BUBBA. Well, now that you ask there are a couple of things... *(He sees* **BEATRICE**, *jumps to his feet, picks up the flowers, moves towards her and hands her the flowers, as* **AUDRINA** *stands.)* Ahhh, for you my vision of loveliness.

BEATRICE. Oh Wilberforce, they're beautiful.

BUBBA. Not as beautiful as you. Would you care for a little bubbly on the beach?

BEATRICE. I'd love to, but I'll need to put these in water first. Perhaps you'd care to help me Wilberforce. *(Moves up stage followed by* **BUBBA**, *then stops and turns.)* Oh, by the way Ms. Brown, I almost forgot why I came in here. I'm very sorry, but I do believe the wedding is off. Would you please inform Madame Coco.

BUBBA. Madame Coco will be so-o-o-o-o disappointed.

AUDRINA. I'm sorry to hear that.

BEATRICE. Thank you. *(Exits up left followed by* **BUBBA**.)

> *(***AUDRINA** *heads to the office as* **DOUGLAS** *enters from room 7, closing the door behind him. He is still wearing swim trunks, a swim shirt and flip-flops.)*

DOUGLAS. Ah, the fair and beautiful Audrina Brown.

AUDRINA. *(Now at the left end of the reception counter, laughing.)* Do you always say things like that?

DOUGLAS. *(Crosses right to the left end of the counter.)* Why are you laughing? I'm sure you get compliments like that all the time. I find you extremely personable and attractive.

AUDRINA. Mr. DuPont, flattery will get you everywhere. *(**DOUGLAS** reacts.)* Well, not everywhere.

DOUGLAS. A guy can hope. Well, I'm off to the pool. Before I go I wanted to ask if I could get a couple more towels.

AUDRINA. Of course, but if you've got a minute, would you mind if I asked you a question.

DOUGLAS. If it keeps me here with you, ask away.

AUDRINA. I'm curious, are you here on business or pleasure?

DOUGLAS. A little bit of business, and now that I've met you, a great deal of pleasure.

AUDRINA. You are incorrigible.

DOUGLAS. I hope so.

AUDRINA. Well, I hope you're having a good time, despite the earlier incident on the beach.

DOUGLAS. I can assure you I'm having a delightful time, especially since I've met you.

AUDRINA. Does your business have to do with hotels?

DOUGLAS. It can sometimes. I do have to travel.

AUDRINA. You don't want to talk about it do you?

DOUGLAS. Not really. Especially when I'd much rather talk about you having a drink with me later.

AUDRINA. Really, you haven't asked me.

DOUGLAS. I'm asking you right now.

AUDRINA. Then the answer is a definite...maybe.

DOUGLAS. That's good enough for me...for now. I'll check back in later and try to turn maybe into yes. *(Exits down left.)*

> *(**CANDY** enters from the office in time to see him exit and starts working on the computer.)*

TRACI. *(Enters from up left and crosses right to* **AUDRINA.***)* Ms. Brown, I am so embarrassed. I want to apologize for my behavior this morning. I can't make excuses, but I really was very upset.

AUDRINA. It's alright, I understand.

TRACI. I have to tell you that I'm afraid the wedding is definitely off. Peter called and told me he has left the hotel and he doesn't know if he'll return.

CANDY. *(Looks up.)* What do you mean left the hotel, he was just here.

TRACI. What?

CANDY. He just left to go to the pool.

AUDRINA. That wasn't Peter Mudd, that was Douglas DuPont.

CANDY. Who's Douglas DuPont?

AUDRINA. He's the guy in room seven.

TRACI. Then where's Peter?

AUDRINA. He's in room twenty-two.

CANDY. Oh dear.

AUDRINA. What's wrong?

CANDY. I've really messed up. I told your mother that your fiancé was coming on to me, but it wasn't him, it was that DuPont guy, so you see, your fiancé has done absolutely nothing wrong. I'm so sorry.

TRACI. Oh no! What have I done?

AUDRINA. Why don't you call him and try to explain.

TRACI. That's a great idea. *(Whips out her cell phone and calls.)*

CANDY. I just knew it was a bad idea. I didn't know the rooms were switched.

TRACI. *(On her phone.)* Peter, oh Peter, I'm so sorry, please forgive me, I've made a terrible mistake. *(Pauses.)* I know you don't. I'll explain it all later. *(Pauses.)* Just please come back, I love you and want to marry you. *(Pauses.)* You do? *(Pauses.)* Hurry darling.

(Enter **BEATRICE** *and* **BUBBA** *from up left.)*

Mother, the wedding is on.

BEATRICE. Are you sure?

TRACI. Oh, he's so wonderful. He said he can't wait to marry me.

AUDRINA. Congratulations Miss Traci. Madame Coco will be very delighted. Don't you think so Uncle Bubba?

BUBBA. Thrilled.

TRACI. We'll need to speak with her again soon.

AUDRINA. I'll arrange it and let you know when she's available.

BUBBA. A week from Wednesday?

AUDRINA. Uncle Bubba, why don't we go see if we can find Madame Coco. Candy, after you put the beach bar snacks out, please man the front desk. *(To* **BEATRICE** *and* **TRACI***.)* If anyone needs anything, just ring the bell.

CANDY. *(Holds the bell up and looks at* **BEATRICE***.)* Once. *(Exits to the kitchen.)*

BUBBA. Beatrice, will you please excuse me my dear, duty calls again. I'm looking forward to bubbly on the beach later. *(He exits to the office followed by* **AUDRINA***.)*

TRACI. *(Grabs* **BEATRICE***'s hands and starts jumping up and down.)* I just knew it, I knew it couldn't be true. Peter would never behave that way. I'm going to be Mrs. Mudd.

BEATRICE. Traci, please. Rutherford-Smythes do not jump up and down like hooligans. Now tell me what happened.

TRACI. The guy who came on to Candy wasn't Peter, it was this DuPont guy, Candy got them mixed up.

BEATRICE. There's a DuPont staying here?

TRACI. *(She lets go of* **BEATRICE***'s hands.)* Mother, don't get any ideas. I'm going to marry Peter.

BEATRICE. Very well Traci, but with the wedding plans on and off and on again, I believe I could use a drink. I'll be at the beach bar. *(Exits down left.)*

TRACI. Alright, I'm just going to freshen up a bit so I look good for Peter when he gets back. *(Exits up left.)*

> *(Enter **PETER** from down right as **CANDY** enters, derierre first, from the kitchen with a big tray in her hands filled with snacks. [SEE AUTHORS' NOTES.] **PETER** stops and watches from down right as the kitchen door swings closed and catches a section of her wrap around skirt. [SEE AUTHORS' NOTES.] **CANDY** twists and turns, balancing the tray, the skirt remains stuck in the door. She turns clockwise till she is facing down stage and the skirt comes off and drops to the floor. She sees **PETER** and quickly lowers the tray, tilting it down and forward, in an effort to cover herself. At this point she is facing **PETER** down right. The contents of the tray spill all over the floor. **PETER** rushes up to help her and picks up the skirt, freeing it from the door.)*

> *(**TRACI** enters from up left. She sees **CANDY** from the side and rear in her underwear and **PETER** holding **CANDY**'s skirt. She marches across in front of **CANDY** to **PETER** and slaps him hard across the face.)*

The wedding is off. *(She turns and exits down left.)* Mother...

> *(**PETER**, holding his face with one hand and looking away, holds out the skirt to **CANDY**, who takes it and puts the tray on the counter as **PETER**, a little wobbly on his feet, exits up left.)*

> *(Enter **AUDRINA** dragging **MADAME COCO** from down right. They stop suddenly as they see **CANDY**, holding her skirt in her hand.)*

BUBBA. Oh Audrina, I like the new receptionist uniform.

*(***CANDY*** *quickly ducks behind the counter with the skirt.)*

AUDRINA. What happened?

CANDY. The wedding is off!

BUBBA. *(Does a fist pump. Then stepping in cadence to the rhythm as if actually doing the "Congo Line Dance.")* No more, Madame Coco, no more Madame Coco. *(This is repeated until he exits to the office. The first time he says "Coco," he stops with his leg out, the second time it is with the alternate leg out.)*

AUDRINA. *(Moves up to the counter and starts to pick up the snacks and replaces them on the tray.)* Candy, I'm not going to ask why you took your skirt off, but please, don't do it again.

CANDY. *(Now wearing the skirt again, comes out from behind the counter and helps* **AUDRINA** *pick up the snacks.)* Oh, I didn't take it off, it just kinda came off.

AUDRINA. How in heaven's – I think I know better than to ask that question. Let's just forget it.

CANDY. That's good because I really don't know how it happened.

AUDRINA. How can you not – never mind.

(Enter **TRACI** *from down left. She is moving quickly and is followed by* **BEATRICE**, *trying to keep up.)*

BEATRICE. You're not going to start throwing things again are you?

TRACI. No mother I am not. This time I have a much better idea. *(She does not break stride and barely acknowledging the presence of* **AUDRINA** *and* **CANDY**. *She marches off up left.)*

BEATRICE. Oh dear! *(Pauses briefly to look at* **AUDRINA** *and* **CANDY**.*)* I'm so sorry but –

AUDRINA. ⎫   The wedding is off!
CANDY. ⎭   The wedding is off!

(**BEATRICE** *makes a feeble attempt to smile, then runs after* **TRACI** *and exits up left.*)

AUDRINA. The magic of sandy toes and salty kisses doesn't seem to be working today. *(She hands the tray to* **CANDY***.)* Ah well, we can't have everything. Can you get these down to the beach bar please.

CANDY. Yes Ma'am. *(Exits down left with the tray.* **AUDRINA** *exits to the kitchen.)*

(*Enter* **DOUGLAS** *from room 7, dressed as before but with his camera / phone in his hand. He crosses right, takes a photo of the entrance.*)

AUDRINA. *(Enters from the kitchen with some towels and moves down to his left.)* More photos Mr. Dupont?

DOUGLAS. *(Turns and sees her.)* It comes with the job, and by the way, it's Doug.

AUDRINA. *(Smiles.)* Okay, Doug. I understand from our receptionist that you're an agent. That sounds interesting.

DOUGLAS. Listen, I would love to be able to tell you why I'm here, but I simply can't. It would be unethical. What I can tell you is that I'm here to make a report on The Lovers' Landing Beach Hotel. So, having said that, if I ask you a few questions, do you think you could give me a few honest answers?

AUDRINA. What a charming way of putting it. As long as I can take the fifth amendment if necessary.

DOUGLAS. Oh it's nothing like that.

AUDRINA. Good, then why don't we sit down and I'll do my best to be honest. *(They move left and sit.* **DOUGLAS** *in the chair and* **AUDRINA** *on the couch right end, putting the towels on the table.)*

DOUGLAS. I'm sorry, I really didn't mean to offend you. When we're done here, I'm still hoping you'll take me up on my offer.

(*The land phone on the counter rings.*)

AUDRINA. Please excuse me. I'd better get that. *(She moves back to the counter and picks up the phone.)* Lovers' Landing Beach Hotel. Oh, I'm so glad you called, I've been trying to get you for days. The price is satisfactory, but I need some firm dates when you can be here to do the work. Yes, I can hold. *(She cups the phone and talks to* **DOUGLAS**.*)* I'm so sorry, this may take a while, they've got me on hold. Why don't you go ahead?

DOUGLAS. *(Talking over his right shoulder.)* It seems like this is a very popular place with the locals. Why is that?

AUDRINA. You'd have to ask Uncle Bubba about that.

DOUGLAS. Can you tell me about the mystique of Lovers' Landing? It seems to me there might just be something to it. Your brochure claims it all starts with sandy toes.

AUDRINA. I guess that's true. Our guests say the magic begins when they walk the beach.

DOUGLAS. Ah-ha, and the magic of sandy toes then leads to salty kisses and salty kisses naturally lead to... *(He pauses and turns his head down stage. At this moment there is a small noise in the office which distracts* **AUDRINA** *who, still with the phone to her ear, takes a step or two just into the office, and so does not hear* **DOUGLAS***'s next line.)* well, *(Pauses and emphasizes the next word.)* sex. *(Almost to himself.)* Douglas, you must be an absolute fool. You're sitting here talking to a beautiful woman, you hardly know, about sex. *(***AUDRINA** *returns.)* So, if I'm right, how do your guests feel about it?

AUDRINA. Oh, they love it. They do it every day.

DOUGLAS. Even on the beach?

AUDRINA. Of course on the beach.

DOUGLAS. Every day? Are you sure?

AUDRINA. Absolutely.

DOUGLAS. That's unbelievable!

AUDRINA. Not really, most of the guests tell me it's the main reason they come here.

DOUGLAS. They talk to you about it?

AUDRINA. Sure. All the time.

DOUGLAS. Everybody does this?

AUDRINA. Pretty much.

DOUGLAS. Well, what about, you know...older people?

AUDRINA. Oh come on Mr. DuPont, nobody's ever too old. As a matter of fact we keep guest books in all the rooms and many of our older guests write about it. They may not have the stamina to do it for very long, but they do mention how invigorating they find it first thing in the morning.

DOUGLAS. First thing in the morning?

AUDRINA. Of course, it's really one of the best times of the day for it.

DOUGLAS. And they write about it?

AUDRINA. Well, some of them do. Of course some of our younger guests think the beach is such a cool place that they do it any time of the day.

DOUGLAS. And nobody has a problem with this?

AUDRINA. *(Laughing.)* Why would they? Isn't that what beaches are for? Excuse me. *(Into the phone.)* Yes I'm here, Wednesday the nineteenth will be fine. 8 a.m. will work. Thank you. *(She hangs up and moves left back to the couch.)* Sorry about that. Now, where were we?

DOUGLAS. I must say this place is full of surprises.

AUDRINA. We like to think so. Do you have any more questions?

DOUGLAS. As a matter of fact I do. Are we on for that drink and perhaps a walk on the beach?

AUDRINA. You don't give up do you.

DOUGLAS. Not when I meet someone as beautiful as you.

AUDRINA. I guess a little fresh air would do me good.

DOUGLAS. Great! Thanks for taking the time to talk with me.

AUDRINA. You're welcome. I have some paperwork I need to finish up before I meet you. Would six at the pool bar work for you? *(Stands.)*

DOUGLAS. *(Stands.)* Wonderful. I'll see you then. **(AUDRINA** *nods yes and exits to the office as* **DOUGLAS** *exits to room 7.)*

> *(Enter* **TRACI** *from up left, now wearing a seductive looking, skirt and blouse or dress with complementary shoes, walking very purposefully. She is followed by* **BEATRICE** *who is trying to keep up.) [SEE AUTHORS' NOTES.]*

BEATRICE. Are you sure you're not going to start throwing things again?

TRACI. No mother I'm not. Now, here's my plan. I'm not going to get mad, I'm going to get even.

BEATRICE. Oh dear. *(Sits on the couch left.)*

TRACI. *(Pacing.)* I'm going to give Peter a dose of his own medicine.

BEATRICE. How?

TRACI. I'm going to put on a little show.

BEATRICE. Oh dear.

TRACI. Believe me, the next man I see won't know what hit him.

BEATRICE. Oh dear. Do you really think this is a good idea?

TRACI. *(Sits on the couch right side.)* Mother, I know what I'm doing. But for my plan to work I need Peter to discover us. Now please, go and find him and bring him back here. He's in room twenty-two.

BEATRICE. Traci, I really don't think...

TRACI. Mother! I need to know if Peter is just playing me for a fool or if he truly loves me.

BEATRICE. *(Stands.)* Okay Traci, I'll do it, but please, don't cause any more trouble. *(Exits up left.)*

> *(Enter* **DOUGLAS** *from room 7 dressed as before and moves right towards the towels. He stops at the table.* **TRACI** *sees him. She immediately smiles seductively, turns left on the couch while crossing her right leg over*

her left, she hitches up her skirt and strikes a pose.)

TRACI. *(In a sexy voice.)* Why hello there. (**DOUGLAS** *looks around then realizes she's talking to him and points to himself.* **TRACI** *nods yes. She stands, moves right and purposefully, in a sexy manner, advances on him.)* You must be the strong silent type. That's perfect.

DOUGLAS. You look familiar. Do I know you?

TRACI. *(Still advancing.)* Not yet, but you will.

DOUGLAS. *(Puts his hands out to stop her and takes a step or two towards the right arm of the couch.)* Wait a minute, weren't you the girl at the pool earlier today?

TRACI. *(Runs her fingers up his chest.)* So you noticed me, mister tall, dark and handsome.

DOUGLAS. What are you doing?

TRACI. What does it look like I'm doing?

DOUGLAS. *(Takes a step backwards.)* I can't believe this is happening...again.

TRACI. *(Takes a step forward.)* Oh, you can believe it.

DOUGLAS. This is crazy. *(Takes a step backward, now with his legs backed up against the back of the couch.)*

> (**TRACI** *takes one more step towards him as* **DOUGLAS** *tries to take a step backwards. His legs are up against the back of the chair. He looses his balance and falls backwards over the back of the chair with his legs up in a V.* **TRACI** *immediately falls on top of him, between his legs as* **CANDY** *enters from down left carrying an empty tray.* **CANDY** *walks slowly towards the right of the chair, stops, bends down and looks at them as* **DOUGLAS** *and* **TRACI**, *still in the same position, look at her.)*

CANDY. Mr. DuPont? With Miss Traci? Have I missed something?

DOUGLAS. Candy, please help me.

CANDY. It doesn't look to me like you need any help.

TRACI. Candy, be a good girl and run along please.

DOUGLAS. It's not what it looks like.

CANDY. Well you could have fooled me. I'm so glad I didn't let you kiss me. *(Exits to the kitchen.)*

DOUGLAS. Would you get off me please?

TRACI. *(Pushing upward lifts herself off the arm of the couch.)* Why, aren't you having fun?

DOUGLAS. If I'd met you earlier I might have, but things have changed. *(Now sliding off and standing in front of the couch as **TRACI** advances on him around the right side of the chair.)* Please listen to me. You don't know what you're doing. *(He backs up around the coffee table towards center stage.)*

TRACI. *(Still advancing.)* Oh, you're so wrong. I know exactly what I'm doing.

DOUGLAS. *(Stops now center stage.)* Look, I'm really very flattered, but you've got to understand. You're not really attracted to me. You've simply been seduced by the mystique of Lovers' Landing, you know...sandy toes and salty kisses.

> *(Noises off. A door closing up left. **TRACI** believes it to be **PETER**, and takes immediate action. She grabs **DOUGLAS** and gives him a huge kiss as **BEATRICE** enters upstage left and moves towards **TRACI**.)*

BEATRICE. Traci?

TRACI. Where's Peter?

BEATRICE. He's not in his room.

DOUGLAS. Who's Peter?

TRACI. Mother, you have to find him.

DOUGLAS. This is your mother?

TRACI. Did you check the beach bar?

BEATRICE. Well, no.

DOUGLAS. Who's Peter?

TRACI. Mother, please go see if Peter's at the beach bar and bring him back here.

DOUGLAS. Who's Peter?

BEATRICE. Traci, I'm not sure –

TRACI. Mother!

BEATRICE. Okay Traci. *(Exits down left.)*

DOUGLAS. Who's Peter?

TRACI. A guy I know, now where were we?

DOUGLAS. We weren't anywhere.

TRACI. We will be soon. *(She takes one more step towards him as **DOUGLAS** tries to take a step backwards towards the chair. **TRACI** pushes him onto the chair and jumps on top of him as **BUBBA** enters from downstage right. He is now wearing dress shorts, same collared shirt with a bow tie, socks pulled up to his calfs with tennis shoes and his hair is slicked back. He sees them and crosses left behind the chair.)*

BUBBA. I know this is the home of sandy toes and salty kisses, but this is a hotel you know. Can I rent you a room?

TRACI. *(Stands and faces **BUBBA** as **DOUGLAS** sits up.)* Mr. Brown, oh dear. Is that you?

BUBBA. Last time I looked it was. So, I take it the wedding is on again?

DOUGLAS. What wedding?

BUBBA. *(Indicates both them.)* Your wedding.

DOUGLAS. WHAT?

TRACI. He means my wedding

DOUGLAS. *(Stands.)* You're getting married?

TRACI. Maybe.

BUBBA. Maybe! What's that supposed to mean?

TRACI. Oh this is all Peter's fault. Excuse me I need to talk to my mother. *(Exits down left.)*

BUBBA. You're not the fiancé?

DOUGLAS. No.

BUBBA. Let me introduce myself, I'm Bubba Brown. And you are?

DOUGLAS. Douglas DuPont. I remember you, you run the bingo games.

BUBBA. You're the guy in room seven?

DOUGLAS. Yes. Who was that woman?

BUBBA. Do you always go around kissing women you don't know?

DOUGLAS. Not until I arrived here.

BUBBA. Then may I suggest you curb your animal instincts. We run a respectable hotel here.

DOUGLAS. Respectable hotel? With everything that's going on around here?

BUBBA. There's nothing going on around here.

DOUGLAS. I would have thought the locals would be in an uproar with all the, um, how should I word this – extra curricular activity going on here.

BUBBA. They'd be in an uproar if we stopped. They love it. Many of them participate and besides, it's good for tourism.

DOUGLAS. Good for tourism?

BUBBA. Sure, the sheriff doesn't think we're doing anything wrong.

DOUGLAS. The sheriff takes part?

BUBBA. Well, not him personally, but his mother does.

DOUGLAS. His mother?

BUBBA. Absolutely. So, as you can see, it's all above board and out in the open.

DOUGLAS. Out in the open! I'll say.

BUBBA. I don't see why you're so concerned. As I said, we've got nothing to hide.

DOUGLAS. That's putting it mildly.

BUBBA. I'm glad you agree. Well, now that we've got that cleared up please excuse me. I've got a date with destiny. *(Exits up left.)*

(**AUDRINA** *enters from the office, unseen by* **DOUGLAS** *She stops in the doorway as she overhears his conversation.*)

DOUGLAS. *(Takes out his cell phone and dials.)* Hey, it's me. This is even bigger than I thought. There's stuff going on around here that you wouldn't believe. Even the local sheriff is involved. *(Pauses.)* Oh no, I'm not even close to completing the investigation. I have a feeling there's more going on here than meets the eye. This is going to be huge. *(Pauses.)* Yes of course I'll document everything. *(Pauses.)* Right, I'll keep you posted. Bye. *(Picks up the towels and exits to room 7.)*

BUBBA. *(Enters from up left.)* Oh, hi Audrina.

AUDRINA. Uncle Bubba, do you have a minute?

BUBBA. This isn't going to take long is it? I'm really quite busy.

AUDRINA. *(Looks him up and down.)* Yes, I can see that.

BUBBA. What? Do you have a problem with my spiffing up a little?

AUDRINA. Of course not.

BUBBA. Well for your information I was looking for Beatrice, but she doesn't appear to be in her room.

AUDRINA. Uncle Bubba please, we really need to talk. Can we sit down for a minute? (**AUDRINA** *sits on the chair and* **BUBBA** *sits on the couch.*) First, I had a very strange phone call a few minutes ago. A gentleman said he wanted to leave a message for Pegasus. Left me his name and number and then hung up. Do you know what this is about?

BUBBA. Oh dear. Candy was supposed to be taking those calls.

AUDRINA. Is there something going on around here that I should know?

BUBBA. Well, I was going to tell you eventually.

AUDRINA. So, you know who Pegasus is?

BUBBA. That would be me. I'm Pegasus.

AUDRINA. What? Why Pegasus?

BUBBA. He's the Greek God of horses.

AUDRINA. I don't know if I want to hear this, but you'd better go on.

BUBBA. Well, the truth is – you see – I kind of place bets on the ponies for people.

AUDRINA. So why the alias?

BUBBA. Well, off track betting is illegal in this state.

AUDRINA. *(Stands.)* Are you telling me you're a bookie, running an illegal betting operation, in our hotel?

BUBBA. Well, yes and no.

AUDRINA. What's that supposed to mean?

BUBBA. Sit down please and I'll explain. *(**AUDRINA** sits.)* The way I work it, it's legal.

AUDRINA. But you just said –

BUBBA. Nobody calls in a bet. They leave a message and I call them back on my cell phone.

AUDRINA. I don't get it, it's the same thing isn't it?

BUBBA. Actually no. You see, I've made sure that my cell phone is registered in a state where off track betting is legal. So, as far as anyone knows, the bet is being placed in that state.

AUDRINA. But you're making the call in this state.

BUBBA. You know how cell phones work. Nobody ever knows where the call originates.

AUDRINA. Are you absolutely certain about all this?

BUBBA. Well the sheriff doesn't see a problem with it.

AUDRINA. He knows about this?

BUBBA. Of course, his mother's a regular client.

AUDRINA. She seems to be a regular everything. You know Uncle Bubba, it looks like you've done it again. How do you dream up all of these schemes.

BUBBA. Guess I've just got a creative imagination.

AUDRINA. Or a brilliant criminal mind.

BUBBA. Remember Mark Twain my dear. He said, "There's no distinctly criminal class in America, as long as you exclude congress."

AUDRINA. *(Laughing.)* Oh my gosh, I almost forgot, I overheard Mr. DuPont on the phone telling someone he was continuing his investigation. He even mentioned the sheriff and he thinks there's more going on here than meets the eye.

BUBBA. Oh boy, I thought he was going to go away after our little chat.

AUDRINA. Uncle Bubba, you didn't try to bribe him did you? That would be illegal.

BUBBA. I might be crafty, but I'm not stupid.

AUDRINA. So if everything you're doing is legal, why do we have to worry about Mr. DuPont.

BUBBA. Well, it's not the activities that worry me, it's my pension plan.

AUDRINA. Your pension plan? What's that got to do with anything?

BUBBA. Well, – um, – well – I –

AUDRINA. Exactly how much is your pension plan worth?

BUBBA. Roughly – three million dollars.

AUDRINA. Wow! That's a lot of money.

BUBBA. I know.

AUDRINA. So what's the problem?

BUBBA. Well, most of the money has come from my "extra curricular endeavors" as you call them, and I thought it might be better if the U.S. government didn't know about them.

AUDRINA. You mean you have't declared any of that income to the IRS?

BUBBA. *(Shakes his head no, as* **AUDRINA** *stares at him.)* Well, you know what the Godfather said, "Behind every successful fortune there's a crime."

AUDRINA. Uncle Bubba, that's tax evasion. What are we going to do?

BUBBA. We'll just have to keep a closer eye on him, and find out what he's up to. In the meantime, don't worry, things have a way of working out. Speaking of which, I think I'll go see if Beatrice is at the beach bar. *(Stands.)*

AUDRINA. *(Stands.)* You know what your problem is Uncle Bubba?

BUBBA. I only have one? *(Gives* **AUDRINA** *a kiss on the head, then moves down left. He stops and turns towards* **AUDRINA**.*)* Smile girl, I'm not wearing orange yet. *(Exits down left.)*

AUDRINA. *(Moves behind the counter.)* Oh Uncle Bubba, what am I going to do with you.

PETER. *(Enters from up left and moves towards the counter.)* Hello, Audrina isn't it?

AUDRINA. Yes, it is. What can I do for you Mr. Mudd?

PETER. Please, it's Peter. I'm sorry to trouble you. I was looking for a woman who works here, but I don't know her name.

AUDRINA. Ah, that would be Candy. Let's see if she's back from the beach bar. *(***AUDRINA** *rings the bell once.)*

CANDY. *(Peeks her head in from the kitchen door.)* Do you need me?

AUDRINA. Candy, can you come out here a minute.

CANDY. *(Enters and moves towards the counter.)* Sure.

AUDRINA. Candy, this is Mr. Peter Mudd, he'd like to talk to you.

CANDY. *(Shakes hands with* **PETER**.*)* Hi, it's nice to officially meet you. I'm sorry about what happened earlier between you and Miss Traci. I feel like it's my fault.

PETER. I was hoping you'd tell Traci how I ended up holding your skirt.

CANDY. I'd be happy to, but I'm not sure she'll listen to me.

AUDRINA. Sometimes a third party can help. Why don't I go and see if she's in her room and bring her out here. If she's willing to listen, then maybe we can get everything back on track for your wedding. *(Exits up left.)*

CANDY. I just hope we can put it right.

PETER. Me too.

CANDY. *(Suddenly puts her hand to her face and starts squinting.)* Oh dear.

PETER. What's wrong?

CANDY. I've lost a contact. *(She moves a little to her left in front of the kitchen door, then drops to her knees and starts looking around.)*

PETER. *(Moves left and drops to his knees and starts searching.)* Here, let me help.

CANDY. Don't move, I think I see it.

> *(She reaches underneath him, then accidentally knocks one of his arms out. He collapses on top of her as* **TRACI**, *followed by* **AUDRINA**, *enter from up left.* **TRACI** *sees* **CANDY** *and* **PETER** *on the floor together. They stop dead in their tracks.)*

TRACI. He's at it again.

AUDRINA. *(Stays up left.)* What in the world is going on?

TRACI. *(Stomps over to them and makes a loud growling noise.)* Peter Mudd, how could you?

PETER. *(Rolls over and stands up, right of* **CANDY**. *He then helps* **CANDY** *stand up.)* It's not what you think. Traci, please calm down and listen.

TRACI. *(Still fuming looks around and sees the oars on the wall. She takes one off the wall and steps around* **CANDY** *and faces* **PETER** *with the oar at waist height, parallel to the ground.)* Calm down and listen, you want me to calm down and listen to you...you...don't you dare tell me to calm down, you – you miserable, philandering, two timing lump of lechery.

CANDY. Oh, you're good. I'll have to remember that one.

AUDRINA. Traci, please, put the oar down before someone gets hurt.

PETER. *(Now standing and backing down right a little.)* It was an accident. I love you. I want to marry you.

TRACI. *(Still threatening with the oar.)* I wouldn't marry you if you were the last man on earth.

CANDY. *(Steps in between* **PETER** *and* **TRACI.***)* Please Miss Traci, it's not what it looks like. *(***CANDY** *grabs the oar and pulls it right. One end gets perilously close to* **PETER***'s privates.)* [SEE AUTHORS' NOTES.]

TRACI. Yeah right. That's what they all say. *(She pulls it back again left.)*

CANDY. He's telling the truth. *(She pulls the oar back again right. This time* **PETER** *grabs the end of the oar to prevent being hit.)*

TRACI. He wouldn't know the truth if it hit him between the eyes. *(She pulls left again.* **PETER** *and* **CANDY** *are still holding the end of the oar.)*

PETER. Traci, I love you.

> *(***CANDY** *pulls the oar right again and this time it hits* **PETER** *firmly in the crotch.* **PETER** *drops the oar, stands for a moment with a look of intense pain on his face, as* **CANDY** *and* **TRACI** *both stand stock still and watch, as* **PETER** *slowly crumples to the floor holding his crotch.)*

CANDY. Oh dear.

TRACI. I hope he's not damaged. *(She moves quickly to* **PETER***'s side and kneels next to him.)*

AUDRINA. *(Moves down and takes the oar from* **CANDY***.)* Let me take this. *(Puts the oar back on the wall.)*

CANDY. Please Miss Traci, listen to him. It wasn't his fault.

TRACI. What?

CANDY. It was an accident, both of the times you saw us.

TRACI. Peter is this true?

PETER. Absolutely. *(He stands and helps* **TRACI** *up.)*

AUDRINA. So, now that we've cleared that up, can we all just relax and get on with a wedding?

TRACI. Oh Peter. *(***PETER** *takes her hands in his.)*

PETER. Oh Traci. *(He kisses her hand.)*

TRACI. I have lips.

PETER. Are they asking for forgiveness?

TRACI. Yes. *(She and* **PETER** *kiss.)*

> *(Enter* **BUBBA** *followed by* **BEATRICE** *from down left who is now wearing a flower in her hair.)*

AUDRINA. ⎫ The wedding is on.

⎬ The wedding is on. *(Sits on the couch right*

CANDY. ⎭ *end.)*

BUBBA. Madame Coco will be thrilled. Is he the groom?

PETER. *(Breaks from the kiss.)* I am.

BUBBA. Who are you?

PETER. Peter Mudd.

BUBBA. The original fiancé?

PETER. The only fiancé.

BUBBA. Okay, but the last time I saw Miss Traci, she was kissing that DuPont guy.

PETER. What?

BUBBA. She was all over him like a bear on a honey pot.

PETER. What?

AUDRINA. Too much information Uncle Bubba.

TRACI. I can explain.

PETER. The wedding is off.

BUBBA. Madame Coco will be so disappointed.

TRACI. It's not what you think.

PETER. Really?

BEATRICE. Traci has done nothing wrong. She was simply trying to make you jealous, you idiot.

TRACI. Mother, please do not call Peter an idiot.

CANDY. *(Tucks her feet under her, and pretends to be eating popcorn while watching T.V.)* Oh my, this is better than any of those dating shows I've watched on T.V.

TRACI. Peter, mother's right. I was just so angry at you. But believe me, I love you.

PETER. You have a funny way of showing it.

BEATRICE. Young man, if my daughter says she loves you she loves you. Now, take it or leave it.

BUBBA. Beatrice, you're so – forceful.

BEATRICE. Why thank you Wilberforce.

AUDRINA. Peter, Traci, maybe you need a little time to yourselves to work this out.

TRACI. Peter I shouldn't have done it. He means nothing to me, I was just using him to get to you.

CANDY. *(Still miming eating popcorn.)* Yep, they do that on T.V. too.

> *(***PETER*** *grabs* ***TRACI*** *and kisses her.)*

Awww... The wedding's on again.

BUBBA. Madame Coco will be thrilled – again!

BEATRICE. Speaking of Madame Coco it looks like we'll need to talk with her again as soon as possible.

AUDRINA. I'm sure that can be arranged. Can't it Uncle Bubba?

BUBBA. Audrina dear, would you by any chance like me to go and find her?

AUDRINA. Why yes, I would, that would be wonderful.

BUBBA. I thought you might. *(Turns to ***BEATRICE*** and takes her hands in his.)* I shall count the moments till we meet again. Adieu. *(Exits down right with a flourish.)*

BEATRICE. Oh my!

AUDRINA. *(Laughing.)* My uncle is quite the character. Perhaps while we're waiting for Madame Coco, we should all sit down.

> *(***AUDRINA*** *sits in the chair,* ***PETER*** *sits right,* ***TRACI*** *center and* ***BEATRICE*** *left, on the couch, as* ***CANDY*** *goes back behind the reception counter and leans forward with her elbows on the counter and cupping her face in her hands, listens intently.)*

TRACI. Mother I'm so happy you recognize that Peter and I are perfect for each other, and that you finally approve of the wedding.

BEATRICE. Traci, it's not that I ever disapproved of the wedding. I just thought you were rushing into things.

PETER. You know Beatrice, I don't think I've ever seen you so relaxed.

TRACI. Peter's right Mom, something's different. This place, or maybe someone here is rubbing off on you.

BEATRICE. Things do not rub off on Rutherford-Smythes. However, we do have the ability to adapt to changing circumstances and certain people.

CANDY. *(Straightens up and in a sing-song voice.)* It's Bubba!

> *(They all look at **CANDY** who covers her mouth with her hand and says a silent "oops.")*

BEATRICE. Young lady, if you are referring to Wilberforce – *(She pauses, softens and giggles.)* – you may just be right.

AUDRINA. Candy, don't you have things to do in the office?

CANDY. *(Pauses.)* Nope. *(**AUDRINA** glares at **CANDY**.)* Oops, I just remembered, yep. *(Exits to the office.)*

BUBBA. *(Now dressed as **MADAME COCO** enters from down right and moves up to just below the chair.)* Is the wedding still on?

AUDRINA. *(Stands.)* What Madame Coco means is she is so happy that she can continue to assist you with your wedding plans. Peter, may I introduce you to Madame Coco.

PETER. Madame Coco, it's a pleasure to meet you. I'm Traci's fiancé.

BUBBA. Thank you. You must be happy to be marrying into this family. Not only do you have a lovely future wife, but such an attractive mother-in-law.

AUDRINA. *(Gives **BUBBA** a "look.")* Thank you Madame Coco.

PETER. I can't wait. But as the planning of the wedding is really girl's stuff, I'll leave it in your capable hands. Traci my love, *(Kisses her hand.)* I'll see you in a little while. I'm off to get a cold beer. See you all later. *(Exits down left.)*

> *(**BUBBA** is about to sit in the chair with his knees wide apart, when he sees **AUDRINA** frowning. He quickly adapts, puts his knees together and sits as daintily as he can, placing his fingertips on his knees, and grins at **AUDRINA**, who gives him a smile of approval as she perches on the upstage arm of the chair.)*

TRACI. Madame Coco, I've definitely decided I want the thousand rose petals.

BUBBA. That can be expensive and very labor intensive for Mr. Brown.

BEATRICE. Perhaps Traci we could do something else and save Wilberforce all that work.

TRACI. Mother, it's what I want!

AUDRINA. I can assure you it won't be a problem, after all, it's what he's paid to do.

BUBBA. Even though the poor man hasn't had a raise in years, I'm sure he'd be delighted to do it for you Mrs. Rutherford-Smythe.

BEATRICE. Oh, he's such a gentleman.

BUBBA. Yes, he does have a certain charm.

TRACI. I can't wait, it will define the wedding. After all mother, I don't believe the Cabot-Lodges have ever had rose petals raining down.

BEATRICE. That's certainly a very good point Traci.

AUDRINA. Now that that's settled, was there anything else?

TRACI. How many people does the wedding chapel hold?

BUBBA. How crowded do you want it to be?

AUDRINA. What Madame Coco means is the chapel can hold most wedding parties and we can accommodate as many guests as necessary on chairs under umbrellas on three sides of the chapel itself.

BEATRICE. I want you all to know that after my delightful walk with Wilberforce, I definitely approve of all the guests going barefoot. As a matter of fact, I highly recommend it.

CANDY. *(Enters from the office.)* Excuse me for interrupting, but the sheriff just called and said it was super important that he speak privately with Audrina and Mr. Brown. He's on his way over here right now.

AUDRINA. *(Stands.)* Oh dear. This sounds important. I'm so sorry, but I think perhaps we're going to have to cut this meeting short.

BEATRICE. *(Stands.)* We understand. Anyway, we have discussed the most important details already.

TRACI. *(Stands.)* I'm so excited. Thank you Madame Coco. It's going to be wonderful.

AUDRINA. Thank you for understanding. We will be available later if you need us.

BUBBA. *(Under his breath.)* I'm not going to wear this dress again.

BEATRICE. What?

BUBBA. *(Runs his hand through the wig.)* I said my hair's a mess again. Please, excuse me. *(Exits down right.)*

AUDRINA. If you need anything Candy will be here. *(Exits to the office.)*

> **(CANDY** *picks up the bell and holds up one finger.)*

TRACI. Mother, I can't wait to tell Peter about our plans. I'll see you in a little while. *(Gives her a quick peck on the cheek and then exits down left.)*

CANDY. *(Crosses left towards* **BEATRICE.***)* Oh good we're alone. I've been wanting to talk to you. It's about the money.

BEATRICE. I'd really rather not.

CANDY. Please listen. I feel terrible about taking the money and all the problems it caused. I want to give it back to you.

BEATRICE. That's really not necessary. If I hadn't offered it to you in the first place none of the misunderstandings would have occurred, so please don't feel like it was your fault.

CANDY. Thank you, but I'd really like to give it back to you. Wait here and I'll go get it. *(Exits to the office.)*

BEATRICE. Alright, if you insist.

BUBBA. *(Enters from down right dressed as before, but now barefoot. He moves up towards* **BEATRICE** *and takes her hands in his.)* I had really hoped we could go for another walk on the beach right now, but I just got word that the sheriff needs to see me. Will you be okay for later?

BEATRICE. Of course, I'm looking forward to it.

CANDY. *(Enters from the office with an envelope in her hand and stands on* **BUBBA**'s *right.)* Oh Mr. Brown, you're here!

BUBBA. Not really, I left five minutes ago, but I expect I'll be back soon.

CANDY. I don't get it. Why would you be back soon if you're already here? *(She reaches in front of him and hands* **BEATRICE** *the envelope.)* Here's the money.

BEATRICE. Whatever are you talking about. *(She hands the envelope back to* **CANDY**.*)*

CANDY. You know the money. *(She hands the envelope back to* **BEATRICE**.*)*

BEATRICE. I have no idea what you're talking about. *(She hands the envelope back to* **CANDY**.*)*

CANDY. The money, I'm giving it back. *(She hands the envelope back to* **BEATRICE**.*)*

BUBBA. *(Who has been intently watching the money go back and forth.)* Well if neither of you want the money, I'll take it. *(He grabs the envelope.)*

BEATRICE. Wilberforce, I have no idea what she is talking about. *(She takes the envelope from* **BUBBA** *and hands it back to* **CANDY**.*)* It's yours.

CANDY. Okay, but I tried. *(Exits to the office with the envelope.)*

BUBBA. Do I need to know what that was all about?

BEATRICE. I rather you didn't. *(Takes his hands in hers.)* It was something I did of which I'm not very proud. Thank you for not asking. You really are a most understanding man.

BUBBA. What I am is a man who can't afford to keep the sheriff waiting. Please forgive me but I've gotta run. *(He lets go of her left hand, kisses her right hand, and exits in a hurry down right.)*

BEATRICE. *(Starts to exit up left, thinks better of it, returns to the counter and rings the bell.)* Once. *(She waits about 5 seconds, then rings it again.)* Once again. *(She waits about 5 seconds, then rings it again.)* Once more.

CANDY. *(Enters from the office.)* Oh it's you. Good job on ringing the bell once, even if you did do it three times.

BEATRICE. You're welcome. Listen, I'm so sorry about what just happened, but I didn't want Mr. Brown to know about our arrangement earlier. I really do want you to keep the money.

CANDY. Wow! Thank you. This isn't a bribe is it?

BEATRICE. No, of course not. Call it Candy's tuition fund.

CANDY. You know, I think you're turning into a real nice lady. Maybe I don't have to worry about Mr. Brown after all.

BEATRICE. No Candy, I don't think you do.

CANDY. That's great. If you need anything just...

BEATRICE. Ring once. (**CANDY** *exits to the office as* **BEATRICE** *moves left.* **DOUGLAS** *enters from room 7 wearing khaki shorts, a polo shirt and flip-flops. He closes the door behind him.)* Good afternoon. You must be Mr. DuPont. I'm Beatrice Rutherford-Smythe. I'm sure you've heard of the Rutherford-Symthes from Massachusetts. *(They shake hands.)*

DOUGLAS. I'm delighted to meet you Beatrice from Massachusetts. Are you enjoying your stay?

BEATRICE. I can hardly believe I'm about to say this, but yes, I'm actually delighted to be here, despite my daughter's erratic behavior since we arrived.

DOUGLAS. Really, that's interesting. Some unusual things have been happening to me too in the short time I've been here. Do you think it could have anything to do with the "mystique" of Lovers' Landing?

BEATRICE. I don't know about that, but there's something to be said for sandy toes and salty kisses.

DOUGLAS. Ah – ha!

BEATRICE. Ah – ha?

DOUGLAS. Ah – ha. I'm actually conducting a little investigation on this place. I'm wondering if it's the "mystique," or something they put in the barracuda drinks.

BEATRICE. *(Jokingly.)* You mean like some kind of drug? Or maybe it's a "love potion."

DOUGLAS. Stranger things have happened. Ask yourself, why would a Rutherford-Smythe like this place? My gut tells me that all is not what it appears to be here, and I'm going to get to the bottom of it.

BEATRICE. Mr. DuPont, I am sure that the Browns run a reputable hotel, and as for my daughter's behavior earlier – well – I apologize.

DOUGLAS. Not necessary. I'm beginning to think she couldn't help herself.

BEATRICE. I'm really not sure what you think is going on here, but good luck with your investigation. Now, if you'll please excuse me. *(Exits up left.)*

DOUGLAS. *(Crosses to the drinks table.)* Of course, just beware of the barracudas.

AUDRINA. *(Enters from the office unseen by* **DOUGLAS**. *She watches as he picks up the pitcher, sniffs and examines it. She moves downstage.)* Is there a problem with the drinks?

DOUGLAS. What? Oh – no. *(Sets the pitcher down and turns.)* So beautiful lady, have you made up your mind about that walk?

AUDRINA. Maybe.

DOUGLAS. Well, I'll be in my lonely, lonely room waiting for your answer. *(Kisses her hand.)* Until later. *(Exits to room 7.)*

AUDRINA. Oh my. *(She watches* **DOUGLAS** *go as* **BUBBA** *enters down right. He moves and taps her on the shoulder.) (Jumps.)* Oh, Uncle Bubba, it's you.

BUBBA. *(In* **MADAME COCO**'s *voice and giving a finger wave.)* Would you prefer Madame Coco?

AUDRINA. Uncle Bubba, if you've got a minute we need to get this sorted out. I just caught Doug, I mean Mr. DuPont checking out the drinks again. *(She sits on the couch right as* **BUBBA** *sits in the chair.)*

BUBBA. This is getting serious. The sheriff is right. Who is this DuPont guy and why was he in town earlier asking all the locals what they know about the hotel?

AUDRINA. Candy said he was investigating us.

BUBBA. But why and who is he working for?

AUDRINA. Uncle Bubba, if he is from the government, and I hope he's not, there are one or two things going on here that aren't exactly squeaky clean.

BUBBA. *(Jumps up.)* I've got it!

AUDRINA. *(Stands.)* Got what?

BUBBA. The answer to our problem. His cell phone.

AUDRINA. What about his cell phone?

BUBBA. Give me ten minutes with his cell phone and I'll know who he's been calling and who he works for.

AUDRINA. How are you going to get his phone?

BUBBA. I'm not, but Candy is. She's going to earn her paycheck. *(He rushes to the office door, leaving* **AUDRINA** *standing with her mouth open. He calls into the office.)* Candy, you got a minute please?

CANDY. *(Appears immediately.)* Sure, what's up?

BUBBA. Come and join us for a minute. *(He moves left, followed by* **CANDY**. *They sit.)* Now Candy, we need to find out just who Mr. DuPont is working for, and why he's investigating the Lovers' Landing Beach Hotel, and I think you can help.

CANDY. Me! What can I do?

BUBBA. We need you to get his cell phone away from him so I can have a look at it.

CANDY. Isn't that stealing?

BUBBA. No it's borrowing. I only need it for about five to ten minutes. Then we'll give it back.

CANDY. I guess that's okay, but how am I supposed to do that? He always has it in his pants pocket.

AUDRINA. Yes Uncle Bubba, how do you propose she does that?

BUBBA. Well, I thought – you know – Candy could use her feminine wiles to distract him.

CANDY. Oh, Mr. Brown I don't think I have any wiles, and even if I do, there's no way I'm going anywhere near his pants pocket.

AUDRINA. It's alright Candy, you don't have to do anything. I'll get his phone.

BUBBA. *(Laughing.)* I suppose you're going to use your wiles?

AUDRINA. No Uncle Bubba, I'm going to use my brain.

BUBBA. Your brain?

AUDRINA. Yes Uncle Bubba, my brain. You two get out of sight in the office and watch the master at work.

*(***BUBBA** *and* **CANDY** *exit to the office.)*

(*Primps a little and knocks on the door of room 7.*
DOUGLAS *opens the door.*) I'm a little early, but it
looks like a rain storm may be heading our way. I was
wondering if you were ready for our walk on the beach.

DOUGLAS. Yes, yes and yes!

AUDRINA. Good let's go. (**DOUGLAS** *closes the door and they
move 2 or 3 steps right when* **AUDRINA** *suddenly stops.*)
Oh, there's just one thing. It's a personal rule of mine,
but walking the beach for me is about peace and quiet
and communing with nature. No cell phones, please.

DOUGLAS. I think that's a wonderful rule. I'll just plug it in
in my room. (*Takes it out of his pants pocket.*)

AUDRINA. Here, give it to me. There's a charging station
right here. (**DOUGLAS** *hands her the phone as* **AUDRINA**
moves behind the desk.) It'll be perfectly safe.

DOUGLAS. Thank you. Are we ready?

AUDRINA. Just one more thing. (*She takes her shoes off, and
points to his. They move down right and drop their
shoes in the tray.*)

DOUGLAS. Sandy toes?

> (**AUDRINA** *nods her head yes, puts her arm
> in* **DOUGLAS**'s *and they cross left and exit as*
> **BUBBA** *and* **CANDY** *enter from the kitchen.*
> **CANDY** *picks up the phone and hands it to*
> **BUBBA.**)

BUBBA. (*Punches a button.*) Oh good, he didn't lock it, that
makes it a piece of cake.

CANDY. Don't forget to check his notes.

> (*Enter* **BEATRICE** *wearing the same sun dress,
> but now wearing, hoop earrings, bangle
> bracelets and barefoot. She is followed by*
> **TRACI** *from up left.*)

TRACI. Mother, I'm afraid Peter can't meet us right now
to discuss the plans. He just got a call from his office,
some emergency they need him for, so he'll be busy for
awhile. (*Sits on the couch left.*)

BEATRICE. That's alright dear, we can do it later. *(Crosses to the counter.)* Hello Wilberforce, how did your meeting go with the sheriff?

BUBBA. *(Looks up.)* Beatrice, oh my don't you look – I would love to go for our walk right now, but I have something I need to do here and I don't have much time. Candy, could you please entertain our guests for a few minutes, this shouldn't take too long. Please, excuse me. *(Exits to the office.)*

> *(**CANDY** moves out from behind the counter and starts dancing, watched by **BEATRICE** and **TRACI**.)*

BEATRICE. Whatever are you doing?

CANDY. Entertaining you.

TRACI. Well, you are entertaining, but I think Mr. Brown meant for you to talk to us.

BEATRICE. Exactly, now come sit down and tell me what is going on. Wilberforce seemed a little anxious. Is everything alright? *(**BEATRICE** sits in the chair and **CANDY** sits on the couch right.)*

CANDY. Well, the truth is we're not sure.

TRACI. Not sure about what?

BEATRICE. If it has anything to do with Wilberforce I insist that you tell us right now.

> *(**CANDY** motions for them to lean in towards her. **BEATRICE** and **TRACI** look at each other, shake their heads, but then both lean in towards **CANDY** at the same time.)*

CANDY. We're trying to find out why Mr. DuPont is here.

> *(**TRACI** and **BEATRICE** sit back up.)*

TRACI. Maybe he needed a place to stay? This is a hotel after all.

> *(**CANDY** motions for them to lean in again. **BEATRICE** and **TRACI** look at each other, roll*

their eyes, but then both lean in towards
CANDY *at the same time.)*

CANDY. Well I caught him taking tons of pictures and making notes in his cell phone.

> *(**TRACI** and **BEATRICE** sit back up.)*

TRACI. Maybe he's a history buff. This place does have a lot of that.

> *(**CANDY** motions for them to lean in again.*
> *(**BEATRICE** and **TRACI** look at each other, shrug,*
> *and then both lean in towards **CANDY** at the*
> *same time.)*

CANDY. Yeah, but he told me he was here doing an investigation on this place.

> *(**TRACI** and **BEATRICE** sit back up.)*

BEATRICE. As a matter of fact, he told me the same thing. It was odd though. He seemed very intrigued with the "mystique" of Lovers' Landing. He seems to think there's more to it than meets the eye.

CANDY. Well Mr. Brown thinks something is fishy and he wants to know exactly what Mr. DuPont is up to. That's why he's hacking his cell phone to see if he's made any calls.

BEATRICE. Oh! My Wilberforce is so clever.

TRACI. My Wilberforce mother?

BEATRICE. Er – I didn't say "My Wilberforce, I said, "Oh my! Wilberforce is so clever.

BUBBA. *(Dances in from the office waving the cell phone in one hand and a piece of paper in the other.)* I've got it, I've got it! (**BEATRICE**, **CANDY** and **TRACI** *all stand as he comes down just above the chair.)*

Okay, okay here it is. *(They all sit except **BUBBA** who is pacing.)* He's a writer. He works for a New York publishing company called, *(Looks at the piece of paper.)* Destinations America. They're checking out hundreds of destination wedding hotels, and rating them one to five stars.

CANDY. And he's checking out this place? Is there such a thing as no stars?

BUBBA. It's not just the facilities, but the romantic atmosphere.

BEATRICE. Is there anything else?

BUBBA. Just two e-mails today, which make me think he really believes this sandy toes and salty kisses thing.

TRACI. Well Peter and I believe in it.

BEATRICE. *(Pauses a moment.)* That's it!

BUBBA. What's it?

BEATRICE. I think I know how to convince him that the mystique of Lovers' Landing is real and this should be a five star resort.

CANDY. Lovers' Landing? Five stars? This I've got to hear.

BUBBA. *(Perches on the left arm of the chair.)* Me too.

BEATRICE. All we have to do is convince him that the mystique is real.

BUBBA. I think I know what's coming and I'm not sure I like the idea of you being involved in this Beatrice.

BEATRICE. In turn, one after another, we will all play along and convince him we find him irresistible.

CANDY. I already tried that and it didn't turn out real well.

BEATRICE. It doesn't have to turn out, as a matter of fact we don't want it to. All we have to do is convince him we're extremely attracted to him.

CANDY. Oh, then I can do that.

TRACI. I can too, this will be fun.

BEATRICE. Just be sure you tell Peter about it in advance.

TRACI. Of course.

BUBBA. You said, "We," does that include you my dear?

BEATRICE. I wouldn't miss this for the world. I've never had an opportunity to participate in anything like this. Most of my life has been spent attending stuffy boring dinners and cocktail parties. Now, for the first time, I get to let my hair down for a good cause. We're going to get your hotel five stars or my name is not Rutherford-Smythe. What do you think Wilberforce?

BUBBA. *(Stands.)* I think you're crazy, *(Moves behind the chair.)* but for a chance at five stars and to put this place on the map, I'm in.

BEATRICE. Now, where is he?

CANDY. He's walking the beach with Audrina.

BEATRICE. *(Stands and moves to the right of the chair.)* Alright, now listen up everyone. Here are your assignments. Candy, when they return, your job is to get Audrina away from him and get her in the loop. Then wait your turn. **(CANDY** *stands and salutes her.)* Traci, *(Stands.)* after you let Peter know, wait out of sight around the corner from room seven.

TRACI. You can count on me. *(Exits up left.)*

CANDY. I'll wait in the office. *(Exits to the office.)*

BUBBA. You guys get to have all the fun. What can I do?

BEATRICE. You can duck down behind the counter and be ready to intervene in case he tries to get to his room.

BUBBA. That's no fun.

BEATRICE. Wilberforce, leave this one to the girls.

BUBBA. Ooh, that gives me an idea. Why can't I...

BEATRICE. No!

BUBBA. Beatrice my dear, were you ever in the army?

BEATRICE. No, why?

BUBBA. You'd have made a great general.

BEATRICE. Thank you Wilberforce. I've always thought so too.

BUBBA. *(Takes her hands in his.)* I just want to thank you for everything.

BEATRICE. You didn't get *(Pauses.)* everything. *(Gives him a kiss on the cheek.)*

BUBBA. Oh my. *(Moves behind the counter.)*

(*Noises off,* **DOUGLAS** *and* **AUDRINA** *rushing in from the beach.*)

BEATRICE. Alright, let's get this show on the road. I guess I get first crack at him.

DOUGLAS. Wow, that storm moved in quickly, we barely made it inside.

AUDRINA. They always seem to come in fast like that from the gulf.

CANDY. (*Enters from the office.*) I'm sorry to disturb you Miss Brown, but there's something really important that needs your attention in the office.

AUDRINA. Please excuse me Doug, duty calls. Maybe later?

DOUGLAS. Definitely.

(**CANDY** *and* **AUDRINA** *exit to the office followed by* **BUBBA**. *During the following conversation,* **TRACI** *is peeking around the up left corner.*)

BEATRICE. Mr. DuPont, if you have a moment, I'd love to continue our conversation. (*Sitting on the couch left end, she pats the seat next to her.*)

DOUGLAS. I'd be happy to. (*Sits on the couch right end.*)

BEATRICE. (*Inches right.*) To be perfectly honest, I haven't been able to get you out of my mind.

DOUGLAS. Me?

(*Unseen by* **DOUGLAS**, **BUBBA** *enters from the kitchen and quickly ducks down behind the counter.*)

BEATRICE. (*Inches closer and hitches up her skirt.*) Has anyone ever told you how incredibly attractive you are?

DOUGLAS. You can't possibly mean it's because you're attracted to me.

BEATRICE. How do you feel about a May / December romance?

DOUGLAS. A what? Absolutely not.

BEATRICE. This isn't getting us anywhere.

DOUGLAS. Good, because we're not going anywhere. Wait a minute, have you gone walking on the beach today?

BEATRICE. Yes, why?

DOUGLAS. Your behavior tends to confirm my theory about the Lovers' Landing mystique.

BEATRICE. I know, isn't it wonderful! *(She lunges for him and* **DOUGLAS** *wriggles out and stands.)*

DOUGLAS. *(Takes a step or two backwards.)* I'm sure you're a very nice lady, but believe me, you're not yourself. You'll thank me for this later.

BEATRICE. *(Stands.)* Later? Of course, yes, there is always later big boy. *(Blows him a kiss and exits down right.)*

> *(A sound of thunder and the lights flicker.* **DOUGLAS** *shakes his head and takes a step or two towards his room as* **TRACI** *enters from upstage left, now barefoot and moves quickly down in front of his door and strikes a sexy pose.)*

TRACI. Why hello there cutie-pie!

DOUGLAS. Cutie-pie?

TRACI. I couldn't get that kiss between us out of my mind. I've decided I want you... NOW!

> *(She tries to grab him and he escapes right of the chair.* **TRACI** *pursues him, he moves behind the chair and makes a dash for room 7.* **TRACI** *anticipates him and moving between the chair and the couch, arrives at the door of room 7 a split second before him, and with her back to the door strikes another sexy pose.* **DOUGLAS** *backs away.)*

Why won't you just stand still and let this attraction thing between us happen.

DOUGLAS. There is no attraction thing. I told you earlier, you can't help yourself. It's the mystique of Lovers' Landing. *(***TRACI** *advances on* **DOUGLAS** *and they circle* *again as* **BUBBA** *watches unseen by* **DOUGLAS**.*)* For goodness sake, you're engaged?

TRACI. So?

DOUGLAS. Then behave yourself. *(He is close to room 7.)*

BUBBA. *(Steps into the room from behind the counter.)* Miss Traci? Mr. DuPont? Is everything okay?

TRACI. Yes, of course. I was just talking with Mr. DuPont. Please excuse me. *(Exits up left.)*

DOUGLAS. She has a funny way of talking. *(He is about to reach for his door knob.)*

BUBBA. I'm afraid you can't go into your room right now Mr. DuPont.

DOUGLAS. Why not?

BUBBA. While you were out on the beach, I noticed there were a lot of ants by your sliding glass doors, so I closed them and sprayed ant killer. It's pretty strong, but you should be able to go in, in about ten minutes. I suggest you just relax out here and enjoy a barracuda in the meantime.

DOUGLAS. *(Crosses to the drink trolley.)* I could definitely use a drink, *(Pours himself a drink.)* but I certainly don't know about relaxing out here. I left my cell phone on the counter charging, is it done?

BUBBA. Oh, was that yours? I thought it was Audrina's so I put it in the office. Just a sec. *(Exits to the office. Sound of thunder and the lights flicker.)*

CANDY. *(Enters from the office with the cell phone and comes down to* **DOUGLAS** *by the drinks trolley.)* Here you go. *(She hands the phone to* **DOUGLAS**, *then stands with her hands behind her back, leans forward, tilts her head back and puckers up.)*

DOUGLAS. *(Looks at her a moment.)* What are you doing?

CANDY. *(Breaks the pose and speaks rapidly.)* You know before when I asked you what you would do if I kissed you, you said you'd kiss me back and I said you weren't supposed to do that then I said we didn't have to do it anyway and you said you wanted to kiss me and then I said I didn't want to kiss you.

DOUGLAS. I guess it was something like that.

CANDY. Well, now I want to kiss you. *(Strikes the pose again.)*

DOUGLAS. But I don't want to kiss you.

CANDY. *(Breaks the pose.)* Why? What's wrong with me?

DOUGLAS. There's nothing wrong with you, it's just that things have changed. I'm attracted to someone else.

CANDY. You are?

DOUGLAS. Yes.

CANDY. Well then, you're forgiven.

DOUGLAS. I am?

CANDY. Of course you can't help yourself.

DOUGLAS. I can't?

CANDY. Nope. You've been bitten.

DOUGLAS. I have?

CANDY. You took a walk on the beach right?

DOUGLAS. Yes.

CANDY. It's the mystique of Lovers' Landing. You can't help yourself.

DOUGLAS. Do you really believe that?

CANDY. Well, it's obvious you're attracted to Audrina. I think she is to you too.

DOUGLAS. It is? She is?

CANDY. Do you want me to go find her for you?

DOUGLAS. Yes, thank you. I think I'd like that. *(**CANDY** exits to the office as he moves left and sits on the couch right side.)*

> *(Enter **BUBBA** from down right. He is again **MADAME COCO**. He poses by the sign, primps a little, hitches up his bosom and walks as sexily as he can to the right of the chair. **DOUGLAS** watches in horror as **BUBBA***

     advances. He leaps to his feet and backs away
     up left.)

OH NO!

BUBBA. OH YES!

DOUGLAS. *(Backing away.).* OH NO!

BUBBA. *(Advancing.)* OH YES!

DOUGLAS. OH NO NO – NO NO – NO NO – NO!

BUBBA. *(Mimicking the same cadence.)* OH YES YES –
  YES YES – YES YES – YES!

     *(Enter **AUDRINA** from the office. At this point*
     ***DOUGLAS** has backed away around the back*
     of the couch and is close to the door of room
     *7. **BUBBA** has advanced to behind the chair.*
     ***AUDRINA** crosses quickly left and stands*
     *between them, looking directly at **BUBBA**, with*
     her hands on her hips. She pauses briefly,
     then, with her right arm fully outstretched,
     *she points down right. **BUBBA** shrugs and*
     exits down right.)

DOUGLAS. Who or what was that?

AUDRINA. Trust me Doug, you don't want to know.

DOUGLAS. Audrina, speaking of trust, there's something
  I have to tell you. *(**AUDRINA** motions for them to sit on
  the couch.)* Earlier, when you asked me what I did for a
  living, I avoided answering your question, but now it's
  important that I tell you. I'm employed by a publishing
  company –

AUDRINA. It's alright Doug. I just hope that you write nice
  things about us.

DOUGLAS. That's the problem.

AUDRINA. Oh dear, that bad huh?

DOUGLAS. Not at all, not at all, this place is wonderful.
  You're wonderful!

AUDRINA. And that's a problem?

DOUGLAS. Personally no, *(He takes* **AUDRINA***'s hands in his.)* In the short time I've known you, I feel we've made a very strong connection, and I'd like to get to know you even better.

AUDRINA. Oh Doug, I feel that way too. So why is that a problem?

DOUGLAS. Ethically, I can't do a write up on Lovers' Landing when I'm falling for the owner.

AUDRINA. What does that mean?

DOUGLAS. It means one of us has to find a new profession.

AUDRINA. Ooooh! *(She pauses and looks at him.)* Well, we do have an opening for a wedding planner.

> *(The lights flicker and go out very briefly as the phone rings.)*

CANDY. *(Enters from the office in the dark.)* Lovers' Landing Beach Hotel, the home of... *(The lights come on to reveal* **TRACI** *and* **PETER** *[SEE AUTHORS' NOTES.] kissing up left,* **BUBBA** *dressed as before, and* **BEATRICE** *kissing down right, and* **DOUGLAS** *and* **AUDRINA** *kissing on the couch. She pauses, puts the phone down and puts her hands forward, palms up, to indicate what she sees on stage.)* ... *(Surprised.)* It really is the home of sandy toes and salty kisses.

> *(Curtain.)*

AUTHORS' NOTES

The authors have carefully written the script to enable one actor to play the roles of both Douglas DuPont and Peter Mudd, if so desired by the director. Clothing and a simple wig and mustache for Peter, coupled with Douglas wearing glasses should suffice to differentiate the characters in the audience's mind.

Pages 33-34 – In the authors' opinion, much of the humor in the following sequences will be derived from the speed at which Bubba can change from himself to Madame Coco and back. They recommend that the dress be a single garment with a single zipper from the crotch to the neck into which Bubba can step, place his arms in the sleeves and zip it up. The "bosoms" are built into the dress itself. The wig and sun hat are sewn together to make a single unit, to put on and take off. With a dressing crew member and practice, the change over should be able to be made in less than 30 seconds.

Page 37 – The preceding dialogue should leave Bubba plenty of time to change. The quicker he returns the funnier. So THE SECOND HE IS READY HE SHOULD ENTER EVEN IF SOME DIALOGUE IS LOST.

Pages 40 – This visual segment will take a lot of practice to get the timing right to give the effect of Traci looking as if she will be hit with the mop up to the last second when she ducks under it.

Page 57 – The snacks should be all "dry goods." Packages of chips, nuts, etc. Anything that can quickly be gathered up and returned to the tray.

Page 57 – The surest way to make sure the skirt stays "stuck in the door" is to unfasten the waistband offstage and have a crew member, out of sight behind the wall right of the door, firmly grip and hold onto the edge of the skirt as Candy makes her entrance.

Pages 62 – Traci's outfit should be appropriate for the actress's figure and should not offend the audience. Make it naughty but nice. It should however make the statement that she's "on the prowl."

Pages 72 – The key to safely "crotching" someone on stage lies in the fact that the actor being "crotched" always has his hands on the instrument so as to be in total control of the movement himself. SO – once Peter has his hands on the oar, he makes the movement. Both Traci and Candy, while appearing to move the oar, in fact, exert no movement and simply keeping their hands on it are just along for the ride.

Page 93 – If a single actor is playing both the roles of Peter and Douglas, then a body double for Peter would have to have his back to the audience as he kisses Traci.

FURNITURE AND PROPERTIES

ACT I – ON STAGE

A shoe tray under the sign	IN IT:	Several pairs of flip-flops
A drinks trolley	ON IT:	A pitcher of "Barracudas"
		Several small sample glasses
		An ice bucket
The reception counter	ON IT OR BEHIND IT:	One land line phone on a cradle
		One cell phone
		Pens and paper
		A computer
		A call bell
		Room keys
		Registration cards
		Spray can of air freshener
Upstage wall	ON IT:	Two crossed oars or paddles
Low back chair		
Couch		
Coffee table	ON IT:	Magazines

ACT I – OFFSTAGE

Yellow rubber gloves	Candy
Bucket and mop	Candy
Two small wheeled suitcases	Candy
Small carry-all bag	Candy
Large floppy hat	Candy
Carry on wheeled bag	Douglas
Coffee mug	Bubba
Towel	Douglas
File folder	Audrina
Note in an envelope	Candy
Overnight bag	Peter

Envelope with money	Beatrice
Wedding brochure folder	Beatrice
Sign: RING ONCE	Candy
Colander	Candy
Driftwood and dead fish	Traci
Oven mitt	Candy
Barbecue tongs	Candy

ACT II – OFFSTAGE

Bouquet of flowers	Bubba
Large tray with snacks	Candy
Towels	Audrina
Flower for her hair	Beatrice
Sheet of paper	Bubba

PERSONAL

Purse with car keys	Beatrice
Purse with $100 bill	Beatrice
Notes (in bra)	Candy
Cell phone	Douglas

COSTUMES

CANDY

Wrap around skirt
V-neck blouse
Flip-flops
Simple jewelry
Slip or lacy type under garment

AUDRINA

Casual dress or skirt and blouse
Sandals
Simple jewelry

DOUGLAS

Khaki shorts
Polo shirt
Sandals
Eye-glasses (Only if Douglas and Peter are doubled)
Swim trunks
Swim shirt
Flip-flops

PETER

Sports coat
Collared shirt (No tie)
Pants (Smart casual)
Loafer style shoes (No socks)
Shorts (Smart casual)

BEATRICE

Sleeveless blouse
Blazer
Dress pants or skirt
Dress pumps or heels
Pearl necklace and earrings, watch
Casual sundress
Sandals
Flower for her hair

TRACI

Sleeveless dress
Long scarf
Heeled sandals
Expensive looking elegant jewelry
Purse
Seductive looking skirt & blouse or dress with shoes that complement

BUBBA

Swim trunks
T-shirt
Swim fins
Air tank in harness
Mask
Regulator
Baggy cargo shorts
T-shirt that says "Macho Man"
Calf length socks
Tennis shoes

Ankle length summer flowered dress
Blonde curly wig
Large straw sun hat
Large flamboyant sunglasses
Ample bosom's bra (See Authors' Notes)
Collared button shirt
Dress shorts
Bow tie

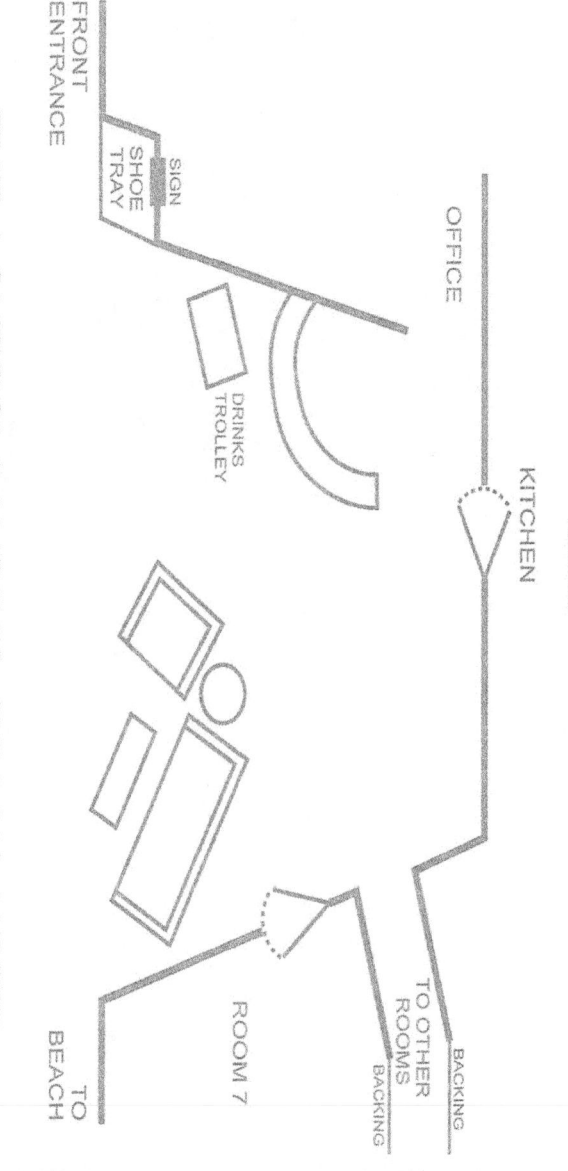

THE LOVERS' LANDING BEACH HOTEL

FRONT ENTRANCE

SHOE TRAY

SIGN

DRINKS TROLLEY

OFFICE

KITCHEN

BACKING

TO OTHER ROOMS

BACKING

BACKING

ROOM 7

TO BEACH